The Promise

The Promise

MONICA HUGHES

SIMON & SCHUSTER BOOKS FOR YOUNG READERS
Published by Simon & Schuster
New York   London   Toronto   Sydney   Tokyo   Singapore

SIMON & SCHUSTER BOOKS FOR YOUNG READERS
Simon & Schuster Building
Rockefeller Center
1230 Avenue of the Americas
New York, New York 10020
Copyright © 1989 by Monica Hughes
First U.S. edition 1992
All rights reserved including the right of reproduction
in whole or in part in any form.
Originally published in Canada by Stoddart Publishing Co. Ltd.
SIMON & SCHUSTER BOOKS FOR YOUNG READERS
is a trademark of Simon & Schuster.
Designed by Vicki Kalajian
Manufactured in the United States of America

10 9 8 7 6 5 4 3 2 1

Library of Congress Cataloging-in-Publication Data
Hughes, Monica. The promise / Monica Hughes. p.   cm. Summary:
A promise made by her parents before she was born sends ten-year-old
Princess Rania to the desert continent of Roshan to
learn mastery of the wind and rain from the old woman
known as the Sandwriter. Sequel to "Sandwriter." [1. Fantasy.]
I. Title. PZ7.H87364Pr 1992 [Fic]—dc20 91–21674 CIP
ISBN: 0–671–75033–x

The Promise

1

$\mathcal{T}$he island of Roshan scorched beneath its white sun, the white sand of its desert enduring the dry winds, as it had endured them for thousands of years, ever since the rain gods had been tricked into giving all their gifts to the twin continents of Komilant and Kamalant, far to the west.

"Atbin, hurry! Atbin!" The words floated up from the sunken courtyard and were torn apart by the wind.

Atbin ran down the carved sandstone steps, his bare feet sure against a surface smoothed by generations of villagers. He could have run blindfolded, the stairs were so familiar to him. The underground house, carved into the sandstone walls of the courtyard, near the oasis of Ahman and the Great Dune of Roshan, was the only home he had ever known. Today he ran faster than usual because of the excitement in his mother's voice, she who was always the calmest and quietest woman in the village of Ahman.

"Where have you been? Your father has been searching for you ever since the sun touched the south wall. Never mind. No time for talk. Hurry, get out of those dusty clothes and into a clean robe. Lucky for you I cut this cloth off the loom and sewed it yesterday. Plain by city standards, I dare say, but new and clean. It will have to do—"

"Mother!" Atbin broke into the chatter that threatened to go on as long as the desert wind. "Mother, the robe will do for *what*?"

Shudi stared at her eldest son, then smacked her hand against her head and laughed, teeth shining white in her brown face. "There, if I didn't forget in all the excitement. Why, we've talked of nothing else since *she* came."

"She?"

"Sandwriter." Shudi's voice dropped to a whisper. Her eyes were round with awe.

"Sandwriter came *here*?" Atbin stared back. The ancient priestess held the whole planet of Rokam in her hands, not only the desert continent of Roshan but also the rich and powerful twin continents of Komilant and Kamalant. She lived in some secret place in the mountain behind the Great Dune and never came to other people's houses. Never, save for one time, when he was very small. The villagers still sang of it.

"She didn't come down *here*. She was up above. Standing waiting when your father went up to water the kroklyns this morning."

"*Sandwriter!* What did she want?"

"That's what it's all about, isn't it? You are to take a message from her to the palace in Malan."

Atbin drew in so deep a breath that he choked. "*Malan?* But Malan isn't even in Roshan."

"Of course not. It's across the Small Sea. The capital of Kamalant and Komilant. The biggest city in the world. And you will actually travel there, my son, all the way from the village of Ahman."

"How? We don't have any money, Mother. And what about a boat? How do I—?"

"Sandwriter will have thought of all that, you may be sure. Now let's look at you. That's a fine piece of cloth, if I say so myself. It may be plain, but you won't find better weavers in Malan, I'll swear. Let me brush your hair. There, that's better. Here's a bag of food, enough for four days. And water bags. And a blanket. Your father has his fastest kroklyn ready for you, watered and saddled. Off you go now. Can't keep Sandwriter waiting. No, give me a kiss first. Behave yourself, for the honor of the village."

With a final pat she let him go. As Atbin ran up the steps that led from the cool underground courtyard to the sunbaked surface of the desert, he saw the aunts and uncles, the nieces and nephews, watching from the shadows. He took a shaky breath. He, Atbin, son of the elder of the village of Ahman, was making history today. His great journey across the sea on behalf of Sandwriter herself would become part of the myth and song of Roshan.

His father's favorite kroklyn, the only means of transportation in this island desert, was tethered outside its stable. He forced it to kneel so he could stow his supplies in the panniers attached to each side of the padded saddle.

The kroklyn's snakelike neck whipped around so that its wedge-shaped head glared at him. It drew back its lips and hissed menacingly, its razor-sharp teeth glinting in the sun. Saliva dripped from its mouth. Atbin paid no attention to its display of temper, but unhitched it, set one foot on its hairy foreleg and scrambled up into the saddle. Once secure, he kicked his left heel against its flank and slapped its shoulder with the reins. The kroklyn lumbered to its feet and set off toward the Great Dune which reared against the sky like a frozen wave to the north of the village.

He hobbled the beast at the foot of the dune and scrambled to the top, his heart beating, not so much from the exertion of the climb, although the slope was very steep, but with awe. He had set foot on the Great Dune only once before in his life, when he came here to be named by Sandwriter on his tenth birthday, six years before.

At the top he drew breath and gazed around. What a holy place it was! Why, from here he could surely see all of Roshan spread out below him, a great brownish desert stretching in every direction to meet the blazing sky. Only to the north, the direction of the sun's path, was the horizon interrupted by the sacred mountain, rosy red and riddled with hollows and caves.

Atbin scrambled down the far side of the dune into the valley that lay between dune and mountain, his heels braking his slide down the slipping sand. Close to the mountain a wind-carved pillar stood sentinel in the quiet valley. These *handars*, whose sculpted shapes stood like frozen ghosts in the desert, were as sacred as the dune itself. He folded his legs and sat cross-legged, his head bowed, until his desert ears heard the faint sound of moving sand.

He looked up, to see *her* standing in front of him. She was a small woman, wearing a brown robe, frayed and patched. Though her face was shadowed by her hood, her eyes seemed to shine from the darkness with a light of their own.

"You are Atbin, son of Shudi and Atmon?"

"As you well know, Sandwriter."

"Do you remember the visit to your village of the young chief of Roshan and Princess Antia from Kamalant?"

"Twelve years ago, when I was four. Yes, indeed, Sandwriter. We still sing the song of the great storm that you—"

"Princess Antia and the young chief Jodril have a daughter—"

"Yes, I know. And a son." Atbin did not want her to think that the people of the oasis were backward in their knowledge of what went on throughout Roshan, or even in Kamalant across the sea. After all, the oasis was the center of the whole world of Rokam and travelers passing by brought the latest news to the village.

"The daughter will be ten years old in two ten-days' time," Sandwriter went on. "You are to ride west to Lohat, the capital of Roshan, and go to the house of Chief Hamrab—"

"*Me?*" Atbin gasped.

"—and tell him that Sandwriter has need of his fastest ship to take you across the Small Sea of Malan. You must arrive at the palace in time for Princess Rania's birthday party and take her my gift."

Atbin's head spun. To talk to the chief of Roshan, to demand a ship, to go across the sea to the palace: it was all too much to comprehend. He felt rather than saw Sandwriter place a small box in his hands. He smelled the scent of the wood, a spiciness that was the smell of the desert when the wind was in the east.

He looked up. She was gone. The wind smoked

along the floor of the valley and wiped out her footprints.

In Malan the tropical rains poured off the tiled roof of the palace and pounded on the marble pavement of the courtyard outside. The room blazed with lightning and Rania started up in bed. As the sky flamed again she could see the fruit trees bending under the wind. Tomorrow the ground would be blue with torn blossoms. The rain came down in silver rods that shattered into white foam as they hit the pavement, but within the palace all was quiet. Or was it? She was sure it was not the storm that had awakened her.

She slipped out of bed and padded across the cool marble floor to the archway leading to the nursery. In the flashes of lightning she could see the shape of Nan, like a stranded whale. In the small bed beyond was her brother, Stefril. She tiptoed across the room to look at him, one hand curled against his cheek, the other clasping his favorite toy, a fearsome stuffed green kroklyn.

He's all right then. So what woke me?

A sudden rasping snore from Nan sent her scuttling back to her own room. A violent gust blew away the rain and then came one of those sudden pauses, typical of spring storms in Kamalant. In the silence Rania could hear the mutter of angry voices, rising and falling like the wind.

She stood close to the carved door that separated her room from that of her parents. Her ear to the crack, she shivered suddenly although the night was warm. Mother and Father *never* quarreled, never.

". . . she should have a tutor *now*, Jodril. After all, she must have a proper education. She is heir to the throne of Kamalant and Komilant."

"But is she? We should be more concerned about Stefril's education. After all, Rania is promised to—"

"No! I won't listen. Rania *will* be queen. She will!"

Rania imagined her mother sitting up in bed, her hands over her ears. She pressed close to the door, straining to hear, hoping the storm would not break out again until she had discovered what the quarrel was all about and what it had to do with *her*.

"Antia, stop it!" Her father's voice was kind rather than angry. "You have to accept it. One day . . . one day soon . . . she'll be sent for."

"I won't let her go, Jodril. She's my baby. Mine. It's a barbaric idea!"

"It is the way of Roshan, Antia. My country—and yours as well since our marriage joined the two nations."

Rania could hear her mother's sharply indrawn breath. There was silence. And then her mother's voice again. "Maybe it'll never happen. Maybe *she* has forgotten all about it. It was twelve years ago, Jodril. She's old. She'll have forgotten. Or chosen someone else, someone more suitable."

In the silence that followed Rania imagined her father shaking his head, maybe trying to draw her mother close to him.

"NO!" Mother's voice rose. "I *won't* let her go! I won't!"

"We made a promise to Sandwriter, you and I, when we wrote our two names in the sand on the Sacred Dune twelve years ago. The promise must be kept. The future of Rokam may depend upon it."

"A promise! What promise? I didn't know what it meant. I would never— It doesn't count. It can't. It mustn't."

The storm swept back over the palace, the wind lashing the trees in renewed fury, the rain's silver rods shattering on the marble pavement, drowning out their voices. Rania ran back to bed and huddled, shivering, under the silken covers.

What is it about? What are they going to do to me? I can't ask Mother or Father, or they'll know I was eavesdropping. I know! I'll ask Nan, that's what I'll do. Nan knows everything that's going on in the palace. With this comforting thought she was able to fall asleep.

"I'm sure I don't know what you're talking about, my love. Promises? The only promises I ever heard were the ones your dear mother and father exchanged on their wedding day eleven years ago. Oh, those were difficult days. Your grandfather dying so sudden and your poor mother, my dear Princess Antia, queen before she was hardly growed."

"Yes, Nan, I know all about that," Rania interrupted impatiently. "But you must know *something*. It's important. There was a name . . . something I don't remember. Sand . . . Sand . . . Sandwriter. That was it!"

Nan sucked her breath in importantly and looked over her shoulder, though she knew very well, Rania thought, that no one else would enter the royal suite without knocking.

"Sandwriter! It's been long years since I've heard *that* name." Her voice dropped and she whispered close to Rania's ear. "She's so important that no one talks about her. It's like she doesn't exist, but she's at the center of everything, do you see?"

Rania shook her head. "What do *you* know about her, Nan?"

"I never saw her, though my lady, the queen, did. She's a kind of priestess woman, and she lives in the middle of that dreadful Roshan desert, not fit for a human being, I should think."

"Is that *all*?"

"They do say that she's powerful and can talk to the gods. There was a traitor, Eskoril was his name, tutor to my lady, the princess as she was then. Sandwriter had him killed without laying a hand on him. Called up the wind, whatever that means. I wasn't there, but I heard the tales, oh indeed yes. They say he was found dead in the middle of that desert with his mouth full of sand."

Rania shuddered. "What a gruesome story! But what can that have to do with—?"

"Nurse!" Queen Antia's voice was a cold knife between them. They jumped guiltily apart. "Nurse, we are far too busy for gossip. There are only nine days left till Princess Rania's birthday and her dress not even finished."

And that was that. Nan wouldn't say another word about the mysterious Sandwriter, and Rania was no closer to finding out what had upset her mother the night before.

There were no more raised voices on the other side of the carved door, but once or twice Rania thought she heard her mother crying. Certainly her face was paler than usual and she had dark circles under her eyes, as if she hadn't been sleeping well.

Rania worried, but not for long. Every day was filled with exciting preparations for the party. She ate every delicious meal the palace chef offered her, she did her lessons, played with Stefril, and slept soundly every night.

She woke at sunrise on the morning of her tenth birthday. Already the palace was humming with activity. In the kitchens all the stoves were lit and boys busily turned the spits, watching that the meat did not burn. Servants ran to and fro with enormous pots and dishes from which the most appetizing smells arose. In the main hall a scurry of servants finished the decorating and gave a last polish to the marble floor, a last dusting to the sweet-oil lamps.

All through the morning carriage wheels scrunched on the white marble chips of the driveway that curved around the fountain in front of the palace. By lunchtime almost all the guests had arrived, Rania was bubbling with excitement and Stefril had had to be put to bed in tears.

"Too much for the little fellow. Leave him in peace, Rania, my love. Come and get into your party dress."

The dress was the most magnificent Rania had ever seen. It was of very pale pink silk, embroidered around the hem and on the sleeves with sapphires and emeralds in the form of tiny flowers and butterflies. It was such a very grown-up dress that she was disappointed when she saw, in the mirror, that she looked even younger than usual, thin and pale, with large dark eyes and long straight black hair. She looked like a little girl dressed up in her mother's robes.

"There." Nan shook out the skirt and looked at her doubtfully. "You look like a proper princess, that's certain sure. A proper princess."

"You look silly," Stefril said baldly when he awoke from his nap and wandered into her room. "Not like my Ranie at all."

"Never mind, Stefril." She gave him a hug. "Tomorrow I'll be your Ranie again."

But he's right, thought Rania. It's as if Mother were trying to hide the real me behind all this embroidery. And she remembered a chilly scene when Father had said it was ridiculous to adorn her like a queen and Mother had pressed her lips together and looked at him as if . . . almost as if she hated him. Which was impossible.

Mother came into the room at that moment and a shiver ran down Rania's back in spite of the heat of the day. Her face was as bleak and cold as the blocks of ice imported from the far north for the party.

"Mother? Am I . . . do I look all right?"

Mother smiled then. "You look beautiful."

Father was behind her, splendid in his white desert robes. He refused to wear brocade and gold, saying he was, after all, only a simple desert chief. But he looks exactly as a king should look, thought Rania, admiring his jutting nose, his high cheekbones, and his eyes as blue and sparkling as the sapphires on her dress.

"Aren't we grand, Father. Look in the mirror, see how I look like Mother."

"I would hardly recognize my little girl." His smile seemed forced and her heart sank. He still doesn't like my being dressed up, she thought.

"It *is* my tenth birthday," she found herself saying, as if it were an excuse.

"Of course it is, my child. Come, now. Our guests will be waiting for you."

"Time for the gifts." Rania forgot the coolness of her parents and clapped her hands. "Oh, Stefril, it's so sad that you are not ten years old, too. Never mind. As soon as it's over we'll play with all my new toys."

"Promise?"

"I promise."

It was scary facing hundreds of strange faces for the first time, even though they were smiling and kindly. Rania held her mother's hand tightly as they walked the length of the crowded hall and took their places, Mother on the queen's throne, Father on the chief's, and she on a small throne on the other side of Mother's, newly built by the palace carpenters, carved and polished, upholstered in white brocade.

She hadn't realized that there would be so many speeches. Even though the recent rain had freshened the air somewhat, the crowded hall grew hotter and hotter. The voices droned on and she had to pinch the back of her hand to keep awake.

Most of the gifts, for which she had to give politely enthusiastic thanks, turned out to be boring. A set of castles, a game with which she had no patience anyway, was carved from precious stones, too valuable to play with, and would probably end its days in the Malan Museum. Huge books, gilded and illuminated, made her jaws tighten in suppressed yawns. A bit better were unusual ivory puzzles from the southern provinces of Komilant, and some quaint dolls to add to her collection.

But then, saved till the very last, was something she had not even dared dream of: a tiny caramel-colored pony, led into the hall by its velvet bridle.

"Oh, Mother!" Rania forgot her manners and ran down the steps of the throne to pat the pony. It nuzzled her with gentle lips as velvety as its bridle. She laid her cheek against the side of its face. "Oh, you beauty!"

A ripple of kindly laughter ran around the room. Rania blushed and went back to her throne. The groom bowed and led the pony out to the stables.

"Does he have a name?" she asked the young noble who had brought her this wonderful gift.

"It is for you to name him, Highness."

"Then I shall call him— Let me see— Yes, I shall call him Freedom, for I'll always feel free when I'm riding him. Thank you very, very much."

There was a spatter of applause followed by the silence that falls upon the end of an event. The queen stood and gathered her robe in her left hand. "Come, my dear." She held out her right hand.

Something in her mother's voice made Rania stare. As if by magic the strain of the last days had vanished. Mother's eyes sparkled again and her smile was happy, not forced.

What has she been so afraid of? Rania wondered. Surely not that I would disgrace her today?

She took her mother's hand and together they descended the steps, her father on the other side. Now there would be a reception in the garden and all the wonderful food the cooks had been busy preparing. Her mouth watered at the thought.

Suddenly Mother's hand tightened on hers. Her arm felt as stiff as wood. She stood staring at the main door.

There was some kind of fuss going on outside. A struggle. Someone was trying to enter, but the guards were holding him back. The guests looked anxiously over their shoulders and then back at the white-faced queen. They whispered to each other behind their gloved hands, behind their fans. Mother's eyes were closed, her face the color of the marble floor.

"Mother, what is it? What's the matter?" Rania shook her arm.

Then Father stepped forward and beckoned to the chief guard.

"It's a youth, sire," Rania heard the man mutter. "From Roshan. Says he must see the princess, that he has a gift for her. But his name is not on the guest list."

"What *is* his name?"

"He says it is Atbin, sire."

"Atbin? . . . Yes, I remember. The son of Atmon from the oasis of Ahman. Bring him forward."

"No, Jodril, don't. I beseech you. Don't let him in." Mother was clutching his arm.

"We cannot refuse him. Come and sit down, my love. Rania, take your seat."

Very upright on the throne, her hands clutching the carved arms, Rania tried to swallow her fear. It was obvious that something dreadful was going to happen. But what?

A young man of about fifteen or sixteen stepped forward, shaking off the detaining hands of the guards. He was tall, sunburnt, his hair bleached pale gold by the sun, his eyes blue with the brilliance that she admired in her father's. His feet were bare and he wore a simple hooded robe of creamy homespun. Staring at him Rania thought that he looked as alien as if he had arrived from another world.

The crowd tittered and whispered, but at the tense white face of the queen the amusement quickly died. The guests drew back so that a wide aisle opened up between the main door and the far end of the room where the three thrones stood.

Along this aisle the barefoot youth walked. He bowed jerkily to the chief and the queen and then turned to Rania. As he stood at the foot of her throne she could see the flush of embarrassment on his cheekbones and that his hands, holding a small box, trembled slightly.

"Here . . ." His voice was rough, just breaking. "Here, Highness, this is for you."

Out of the corner of her eye Rania saw Mother move, as if to prevent her, and Father's hand, gentling her as if she were a fractious mare. She took the box and looked at it curiously. It was simply but beautifully made of a wood that gave off a faint perfume as it warmed in her hands. It was a strange scent that spoke of wide spaces and a deep quietness, of a place that attracted and frightened her at the same time.

She suddenly remembered a picnic place, when she was much younger. There was a cliff and she had stood at its very edge, feeling the current of air against her body, wanting to lean out and out until she was like a bird, flying over the abyss, yet knowing at the same time that to do so would be crazy, that she would fall to her death on the stones at the foot of the cliff. She had the same feeling now as she held the mysterious box in her cupped hands.

"Why don't you open it, Highness?" a guest suggested. She jumped and looked up, realizing that she had been sitting staring at it for a long while. She smiled and struggled to undo the intricate knot, but the thong that fastened the box was of hard leather and her fingers could not budge it.

The young man, Atbin, reached into his robe and pulled out a knife. Those guests who saw its glint screamed, and the guards rushed forward. But Father held up his hand to restrain them, and Atbin calmly nicked the thong with the point of his knife and put it away again. The thong fell from the box.

Rania hesitated, one hand under the box, the other

on the lid. What could it be? The box felt heavy, as if it were full of something unyielding. Something quite out of the ordinary. Not necessarily pleasant. And *why* was Mother so afraid?

"Open it, Princess!"

"Yes, open it!"

Now it was a game. Everyone crowded as close to the throne as they could; every eye was upon her and the box in her hand. Playing to the crowd, Rania slowly lifted the lid a crack and peered inside.

"Oh!" She flung back the lid and sifted through the contents with her fingers. "There's nothing inside but *sand!*"

At her side the queen, her mother, slumped to the floor in a dead faint.

2

*R*ania stood in the bow of the flagship of Kamalant's fleet and watched the low coastline of Roshan creep closer. Her hands gripped the railing so tightly that her knuckles turned white. The water foamed as the prow cut through the silky sea. The engine thrummed, and the paddle wheels turned, the water falling silver from their blades. For days now the funnels had belched smoke and the store of wood had grown slowly less as Kamalant dwindled behind them. Now, on the far side of the Small Sea, lay her unknown future.

Rania had promised herself that she would cry no more. All her tears had been shed at home in the palace of Malan. Tears of fear at first, when Mother had fallen to the floor and she had thought she might be dead. But it was only a faint and Mother, pleading the heat, had gone to her room to recover.

The party had continued throughout the afternoon and far into the night, until the candles had twice burned down in their sconces and been replaced. The music, the excitement and the food were all wonderful but, by the time she and Father had said good-bye to the last guest, she could hardly keep her eyes open. She had the vaguest memory of Nan stripping off her jeweled dress, of rolling into bed, of feeling Nan's soft cheek against hers. Then, unaccountably—or was it a dream?—Nan's tearful voice: "My baby, oh, my precious baby!"

The following morning, now fully ten years old, she woke at noon, shook Nan awake, and demanded to be dressed in riding clothes. Freedom was waiting for her at the stables, soft lips searching her palm for sugar balls. The groomsman saddled him and helped Rania mount. He was wonderful, as smooth in gait and as perfectly mannered as if they had been riding together all their lives. She would have liked to stay in the paddock all day, but there was Nan, calling her.

"Come at once, my precious. My lady and your father wish to speak with you. Oh, what a mess. And smelling of horses. Into a bath with you at once. And your hair! It'll take me an hour to smooth out the tangles."

"I wish you would braid it," Rania said between

ouches. "Because I'm determined to ride Freedom every single day of my life, and I can't bear all this tugging."

Nan burst into tears and wouldn't say why. Surely it wasn't because she had scolded when Nan pulled her hair? She had done it a thousand times before and all that ever happened was a scolding back. Today was different. Was it something to do with being ten years old instead of nine? If so, then the party and the presents were hardly worth it. Except for Freedom. For Freedom, she decided, she would put up with *anything.*

Mother and Father were in their private sitting room and Atbin, the young man from the desert land of Roshan, was with them. Rania looked from his nervous face to Father's, which was grim, and Mother's, blotched and swollen with tears. Her stomach fluttered and she felt sick.

"Come, child, sit on my knee." Father held out his arms and she ran to him. It had been a long while since he had time to play with her.

"Once upon a time," he began and she snuggled close. "Once upon a time, when your mother was a young girl . . ."

"Ten years old, like me?"

"No, she was fourteen years old when this story begins. She came to stay with my family in Roshan and we had an adventure together. You remember that Roshan is my country and that one day I will be chief in the place of my father?"

"Yes, and that is why everyone calls you the young chief." She ran her fingers over his knuckles, strong and sunburnt, like the young man's . . . like Atbin's.

"Your mother and I had an adventure in the desert and there we met Sandwriter, who is the wise woman of Roshan. She blessed our marriage and foretold your birth. She is the greatest person on Rokam. It is she who holds the secrets of the wind and the weather and the great secret of Roshan." He put a finger on Rania's lips as she began to ask what the great secret was.

"One day you will find out what you must know. Listen now, because what I'm going to tell you is very important. Long, long ago, Sandwriter was the aunt of my father, Chief Hamrab. She was still a young woman when the *old* Sandwriter called to her to come and live in the desert with her. She obeyed the call and gave up her family, her wealth, her friends, her future husband and children. From that day on she lived with the old Sandwriter, learning all the wisdom of Roshan, the skills of wind calling and cloud telling, of seeing into the future. When the old woman died at last, my great-aunt became the new Sandwriter. Do you understand this story, my child?"

"Of course, Father. But I feel sorry for your great-aunt."

"The story is not finished yet. Sandwriter is getting old herself and she must pass on her wisdom and skills to someone else—"

"Why?" Rania couldn't help interrupting.

"Because without Sandwriter Roshan could not survive. My country would be like a beast without a heart, a tree without roots, a flower without water. Sandwriter is the heart, the roots, the water." He paused and gestured to the young man, who sat silently listening. "Atbin was sent by Sandwriter to fetch the person who is to be her next apprentice, who is to live with her and learn all she has to teach, who will in turn hold all the skills and truths that are passed on to her."

He stopped talking and Rania leaned against his shoulder, looking into his face. "It's an interesting story, Father, but how does it end? And why are you telling it to me now?"

His arms tightened around her, holding her so that she could hardly breathe. "Because the person is you, Rania. Because you are the child who was promised to Sandwriter by your mother and me, even before you were born."

There was hardly time to be frightened, for she was to leave at once. Atbin was to escort her to the strange woman Sandwriter, far across the sea in Roshan.

"Aren't you going to come with me, Mother? Nan? How can I manage without *Nan*?"

Mother hadn't answered, only shaken her head, hugged her and hurried from the room. As for Nan, she collapsed into the nursery rocking chair, threw her apron over her head and wailed. There was no one but Stefril to turn to and he was only four.

"Oh, Stefril, what is to become of me?"

"It'll be an adventure, Ranie. Like school perhaps. Only don't be away too long. When are you coming back?"

That was the question that no one would answer. I must talk to Father, she promised herself. But he was always busy, and perhaps she was afraid to ask, afraid of what he might say.

There were clothes to be packed, the very simplest things she owned, and enough only for the voyage.

"But what about afterward?"

"Sandwriter will see to all your needs, they say." Nan sniffed.

"My dolls . . . I must take my *dolls*."

"Oh, that won't be allowed, my precious. . . . Well, perhaps just one, then, for the voyage only, mind." Nan mopped her eyes.

Choosing was agony, for all of them were her friends. In the end she picked the fair-haired rag doll with freckles, because it reminded her of Stefril. ". . . and I'm going to miss you so much. How are you going to grow up without me?"

"I'll manage. You mustn't worry. And you'll come home soon." At four Stefril was sure of everything.

Saying good-bye to Freedom was the worst agony of all. She had barely got to love him and now—When she went down to the stable, the groom had him saddled, but she refused to ride.

"I can't bear to. He is Stefril's horse now, you know. It's my good-bye gift to him. Will you have them make a little saddle with short stirrups? Freedom's so gentle, he'll look after Stefril, won't you, my pet?"

She stroked the velvety nose and laid her cheek against the pony's. Then she ran through the hot sun back to the palace so that no one should see her tears.

I must know if I will ever see him again, she thought desperately, and while she still had the courage she went to see her father.

"The young chief is in the council room, Highness."

"Alone?"

"He is expecting his ministers at any minute."

"Five minutes then. Just five minutes." She slipped past the guard and closed the carved door behind her.

"You're early—" Her father turned from the arched window that looked out on to the shadowed colonnade. "Why, it's Rania. My dear—"

"Father, I have to know the truth. How long am I to be away from you and Mother and Stefril and Freedom?"

He hesitated.

"Please, Father. Nobody'll tell me anything. They just *cry*." Her own voice broke and quickly he crossed the room and put a comforting arm around her.

"They can't tell you because we don't really know. Sandwriter expects you to stay with her for a kind of apprenticeship of five years—"

"*Five years!*" In five years Stefril would be nine and Freedom would be . . . middle-aged.

"If you have understood the story I told you," Father went on slowly, "you already know the answer. If Sandwriter has chosen rightly, if you are the one to follow, then she will ask you to stay with her forever. To become the next Sandwriter after she dies."

Rania stared in disbelief at his dear familiar face. "Forever? You're sending me away for*ever*?"

"My dear child, we're not sending you . . . as if we didn't care . . . It is not our choice. When your mother and I wrote our names together in the sand, Sandwriter looked into the future and saw *you*, our Rania, as her successor. We made a promise—"

"To an old woman? Oh, Father, would it be so bad just to break one little promise? Not as awful as sending me away forever and ever?"

He mopped up her tears and hugged her tightly.

"Perhaps it won't be forever. Perhaps she will find she is mistaken. That you are not the one." But his voice was flat.

She pushed herself out of his arms so that she could turn and look into his face. "You don't believe that, though, do you, Father? *You* believe that old woman'll have me forever and ever, don't you? Oh, Father, I can't bear it. Please break the promise, *please.*"

"I cannot, Rania. We cannot. The promise wasn't made to Sandwriter but to Roshan. We wrote our names in the sand. We pledged our child to its future. You must understand that I, the young chief, can't betray my country by going back on that promise, however much I might want to. However much it might hurt—"

"Then you don't love me."

"Rania, if you knew just how much— When you've lived in Roshan for a while you will understand. You'll come to love the desert. You'll —"

"No, I won't. Not ever. I hate Roshan. I hate Sandwriter. And I hate you!"

Rania struggled out of her father's arms, tore open the door, and ran headlong through the startled councillors waiting outside.

They've abandoned me, she told herself. I'll never speak to them again. But of course, when the time came to say good-bye she forgot her anger and hugged them desperately. She wanted to say: Don't make me go. But she was a princess, so instead she stuck up her chin and smiled bravely. She kissed Nan and Stefril good-bye and went aboard the ship with

Albin. She waved until they were no more than small blobs of color on the dock. Then the dock itself vanished in the lush greenery and the coast sank below the western horizon. Only then did she go down to her lonely cabin and cry until there were no more tears left.

The journey, aboard the fastest ship in the Kamalant fleet, had taken less than a ten-day. She had spent most of that time in her cabin, clutching her favorite doll, staring fiercely out of the window at the sea and the empty sky. When food was brought to her she ate a little of what was on the tray, but without noticing what she ate. She felt dry, empty, alone. Like a desert.

Now she was on deck, blinking at the brilliance of the sunlight on the waves, watching the coastline of Roshan creep closer. First a low mud-colored escarpment. Then houses, also mud-colored, crammed together on the slope that led down to the harbor. She could see no flowers, no roof gardens. Nothing but dusty houses and a few dusty fig trees.

She had to remind herself that *this* dingy village was actually Lohat, the capital city of the whole island continent of Roshan. What would the rest be like? She knew Atbin came from a village called Ahman, and she had imagined *it* would be somewhat like this. . . .

The sky was a harsh blue in which the sun shone

like a disk of white-hot metal. Standing in the prow of the ship was like being near the open door of a furnace.

"May I get you something to eat, Princess?" Atbin spoke shyly behind her.

She shook her head. "I'm not hungry."

"You should come into the shade. The sun will hurt you. You are not accustomed."

"Why *is* it so hot? Surely not just crossing the equator into the south?"

"No, it is the dryness. The sun is . . . *there*. Nothing in the way."

"How can you endure it?" She looked at him curiously and he smiled, his teeth flashing white in the sun-gold of his face.

"I found Malan hard to endure, Princess. It was so damp I thought I was choking. I could hardly breathe."

She looked away again, across the water to the land slowly approaching. She could distinguish individual houses now. Almost guess at doors and windows. "Tell me, Atbin. Is this . . . is Lohat much bigger than your village?"

He laughed then, a happy, spontaneous laugh. "Why, Princess, Lohat is a big city. Until I saw Malan with my own eyes I thought Lohat was the biggest city in the whole world. My village has six courtyards and each courtyard has three family dwellings in it."

"*So* small?"

"But we're very important," Atbin added hastily. "Everyone who crosses Roshan must pass through Ahman. We see everyone. We hear all the news. We're not backward, Princess. And our water is the clearest and our dates the sweetest of anywhere on Rokam."

"You love your home?"

"It is . . ." His face shone and his brilliant blue eyes flashed—like Father's, she thought. They are Roshan eyes, desert eyes. "It is the most beautiful place on Rokam. Oh, I don't mean that Malan was *not* beautiful. The palace was the most magnificent building I have ever seen. And the food . . . And the beds . . . But, well, you will have to see for yourself. I can't describe it."

As they talked, the shore crept closer. Now Rania could see that the city had an encircling wall in which the houses had some kind of order. There were people moving down by the waterside. But no bright colors. Everything was either white or the beige or brown of the homespun that Atbin wore.

They drew slowly closer to shore, the thrum of the engine and the swish of the paddle wheels drowning out any land sounds. But smells drifted across the water, the smell of heat and dust, dry and suffocating. After a while she was able to distinguish other scents: something minty, a honey-sweet flower, and a spiciness that was like the bottom note in a chord of music, a scent that was tangy and mysterious, the scent of the box that Sandwriter had given her.

Mysterious. The word best described the great island continent of Roshan. Not Lohat. Lohat was nothing, just a village of mud houses. But behind it was the desert. And it was upon the desert wind that this strange spicy scent was borne.

She stood with her eyes shut against the sun-dazzle, the light off-shore breeze on her face, and suddenly she was somewhere else, not on the firm deck of Mother's ship. She was running over sculptured hills of sand, running as in a dream, the sand dragging at her feet. And now the sand was rising in the air, swirling in great columns that threatened to overwhelm her. One column, directly in front of her, grew close, closer, thickened into the figure of a bent old woman, a woman dressed in brown homespun, white hair beneath the folds of her hood. Brilliant blue eyes turned to her. Piercing her.

There was a roaring in her ears and then black-ness . . .

"Princess? Are you all right? Princess?" Atbin's voice in her ears. His arm comfortingly strong around about her waist.

"What?" She opened her eyes. There was nothing but the sun-dazzled sea and the mud houses of Lohat.

"It's not wise to stay in the sun too long. You'll be ill. Come and sit in the shade of the stern until we dock."

Rania allowed Atbin to help her into the shade and comparative cool of the awning stretched across the rear deck. From here she could no longer see Roshan. From here all she could see was their wake, a frothy double line stretching back across the open sea to the far horizon. Beyond that horizon, eight days away, was Kamalant. She shivered suddenly, uncontrollably.

"Are you afraid, Princess? There's nothing to fear here, I promise you."

"I want to go home," she whispered, so softly that he had to lean over to catch her words.

"They say that your home will be with Sandwriter. What an honor, Princess! I suppose one could be a little afraid of such an honor."

"What is she like? Tell me about her, Atbin."

"I have seen her three times, Princess. Which is more than anyone in Lohat can boast. I saw her first when I was a small boy. She rested in *our* house on the day she called up the wind and destroyed the traitor Eskoril. I saw her the second time on my tenth birthday, when she gave me my man-name. Then I saw her last when she gave me the box to bring you."

"Yes, but what is she actually *like?*" Rania asked again, but Atbin seemed unable to describe her in the way one might an ordinary human being.

After all, she thought, how does one describe a woman who can summon up the wind to kill a man, just like that? How could one live with such a person, eat with her, sleep by her? It was impossible to imagine.

She clenched her hands so that the delicately polished nails bit into the palms. It must be all right. Father knows Sandwriter. He is a Roshanite. One day he will be chief of this country. Surely he wouldn't let me go to someone who is . . . horrible. I must think of Sandwriter as a friend and teacher, she told herself firmly. Someone as kind and loving as Nan, though perhaps not quite so fat.

With a gentle bump the ship nudged the quay. They had arrived. Rania had time for no more than a second's panic before she was in the arms of her grandmother, the lady Sufi. She was led down the gangway and into a simple unpainted open carriage, pulled by a single lema.

She reminded herself firmly that Roshan was a poor country, without the resources of Kamalant and Komilant, and that if the wife of the chief chose to ride in a cart pulled by a donkey only fit for a peasant, that was her business. And Grandmother Sufi was a dear, talking comfortably of nothing particular all the way to the palace, which wasn't a palace at all, but a mud house on an ordinary street, whose wall opened on to a courtyard where women were doing the washing.

She was shown a small white-painted room. "This is the same room in which your mother stayed, when she was a girl visiting us before her marriage."

It's comfortable imagining Mother sleeping in this bed, thought Rania, looking around, although it was a strange bed, being made of a wooden frame interlaced with strips of leather and covered with a thin mattress stuffed with wool. Had Mother managed to sleep in it? she wondered, bouncing on it. It was very hard, different from the softly stuffed feather mattress, the pillows, and the silken sheets to which she was accustomed. And what had Mother thought of the plain white walls, the far one of pierced brick to let in light and air? There was a chair, a chest with a washbasin and ewer standing on it, and pegs on the wall for clothes, she supposed. She had few enough clothes. It hardly mattered. But how Nan would have fussed!

She smiled and blinked back tears at the thought of Nan, and walked over to the pierced wall. By peering between the patterned bricks she caught glimpses of a courtyard and pots, with tired and dusty-looking plants growing in them.

"You must stay with us three days, my dear," Grandmother said. "It's a long journey across the desert to Ahman, and I won't have you arriving tired out. So you shall sleep as long as you like and eat as much as you can. You're looking pale, my child. But of course, I was forgetting. You have your mother's complexion. White skin and black hair. And how are your mother and father? And my little Stefril?"

After telling Grandmother all about the family

—which was hard to do without beginning to cry, but she managed it—Rania was introduced to Grandfather, whom she had not seen for five years, when they had visited Malan. He dressed like Father. He looked like Father too, so much so that she longed to climb on his knee and be hugged. But he wasn't Father. He was Chief Hamrab, a good but stern man who treated her as if she were a grown-up and rather important person.

The three days flashed by. To her surprise she slept deeply on the hard bed, her freckle-faced doll in her arms, and was able to eat all the food that Grandmother pressed on her. She went for quiet strolls down the street to the harbor, and up the hill to the best view across Lohat.

On the fourth morning she was shaken awake while it was still dark and dressed in a desert robe of white cloth that covered her from ankle to fingertip. It had a hood to protect her head from the sun and a sort of scarf attached to the hood which she was told she should wrap around her face, leaving nothing exposed but a tiny air hole, should they run into a sandstorm.

"But the wind is from the west. From the sea. I think you will have a good journey," Grandmother told her. "Now eat, my dear. It will be a long day."

But Rania's stomach had tied itself into a knot and she could swallow no more than a few slices of fruit. Grandmother and Grandfather walked with her across the dark courtyard. The door in the wall had already been opened by the ancient doorkeeper and beyond it, in the shadowy street, something enormous and hairy moved.

Rania screamed and drew back, but Grandfather was behind her and his hands were firm on her shoulders, pushing her forward.

"No! I don't want to . . . don't make me . . ."

"Sandwriter awaits you, child."

"But that . . . those . . ." Now she was at the gate Rania could see that there was not one but four hairy monsters, each the height of the wall, snake-necked, savage-toothed.

"Those?" Grandfather chuckled unexpectedly. "They are only kroklyns, child."

Kroklyns? Rania swallowed her panic, remembering Stefril's favorite toy. The reality was nightmarelike, but everyone else seemed to take them for granted.

One of the beasts was forced into a kneeling position, so that its back was a hand's reach above her head. It turned and snarled, teeth flashing, mouth dripping greenish saliva. She shut her eyes and didn't open them again until she had been lifted into the covered litter that was strapped to the beast's back. Then Atbin scrambled up onto the kroklyn's shoulder and settled himself in the saddle in front of her litter, shielding her from the sight of those glaring red eyes and razor-like teeth.

Grandfather reached up to take her hands. "Good-bye, dear child." He pressed her hand against his forehead as if it were she who was important and not the other way around. It was *his* aunt, she remembered, who had left her comfortable home to become the present Sandwriter. Then Grandmother was beside him, blowing kisses and waving good-byes.

With an unexpected lurch the kroklyn got to its feet. Now she was so high she could see right over the wall into the courtyard within. She looked down on the heads of the last of her family and waved good-bye. The four kroklyns lumbered slowly down the hill.

The sun had not yet risen as they strode on their enormous padded feet through the slumbering town. The streets were deserted, the market stalls dismantled and pushed against the house walls. As they went through the eastern gate the sky flushed pink.

In the dawn chill Rania's litter was cozy and the swaying of the kroklyn's stride lulled her into a doze, out of which she woke some time later, gasping for air, sweat trickling down her face and neck. She drew back the curtains to get some air in the stuffy tent-like box, and the heat outside hit her like a blow. The light was blinding.

She could see Atbin's body only as a silhouette, blocking out most of the light from the front of her litter. How could he endure the heat out there? He sat relaxed, his left leg dangling, his heel against the kroklyn's hairy shoulder, his right leg crooked around the saddlehorn, his hands lightly on the reins. She could hear him sing, a continuous wordless drone. She let the curtain fall and sat back among the cushions. She fell asleep again to the same wordless drone.

They paused only briefly for a lunch of fruit and water, not allowing the kroklyns to kneel or rest. "They work better this way," Atbin told her. "If we stop they will expect water and there isn't enough."

Water. She thought about it through the interminable afternoon. She thought of the rain pounding down upon the roof and courtyard of the palace, of the fountain running day and night in the front courtyard, of being bathed, sometimes twice a day, in cool perfumed water. She eased the damp cloth away from her neck and shoulders and remembered how often she had scolded Nan for her continual preoccupation with baths.

When they stopped at last, the kroklyn collapsed front feet first so that Rania screamed and clutched the sides of the litter, afraid that she was going to be pitched out over its head. Another lurch as the rear quarters hit the sand and Atbin jumped to the ground and turned to help her out.

She climbed stiffly down into his arms and he swung her safely around away from the snarling kroklyn. "One moment, Princess, while we water and feed the beasts. Don't wander far. It's easy to get lost."

Rania looked around. Directly in front of her was a huge red rock that thrust itself up out of the golden-brown crust of sand. She turned to see sand and sky . . . sand and sky. One uncompromising circle from horizon to horizon, broken by nothing but this one plug of red rock. How could she possibly get lost?

Stiffly she walked around to the far side of the rock. Here some trick of the rock or the hot air suddenly cut her off from the screams of thirsty kroklyns and the low voices of the drivers. She was alone. Lohat was a day's ride away and eight days across the sea was home. The desert was huge. Silent. Terrifying. With trembling legs she walked the rest of the way around the rock, staying as close to it as she could, until the noise of beasts and drivers once more filled the air. She ran toward Atbin.

"There you are, Princess. See, here is a place for you to spend the night."

It was a small square tent, cheerfully striped in white and red, carpeted with a bright carpet. There were cushions piled up on the far side, and a quilt. Its sides shut out the terror of the desert and Rania sat cross-legged on the cushions, her back against the tent wall, while Atbin served her slices of baked gazelle and fresh fruit that had been packed in wet clay containers to keep it cool. She was almost too hot and worn out to eat.

"Have another slice, Princess. The meat will spoil by tomorrow. Then you will have to share our desert food."

"I'll eat if you will," she told him. He took a slice of meat, rolled it neatly between finger and thumb and popped it into his mouth. His eyes closed. *"Mmmm."* He caught a dribble of gravy on one finger and licked it clean. "My last taste of palace food, I expect." His teeth flashed in the shadowy tent.

"Have another slice," she urged him. "There is plenty left."

But he shook his head. "It wouldn't be fitting, Princess." He got to his feet and gave a jerky bow. "If you're sure you have finished . . . ?"

She nodded and he picked up the dishes and turned to leave.

"Goodnight, Atbin." She tried to keep the tremor out of her voice.

"Goodnight, Princess."

The sun set abruptly and within a few minutes it was dark. Lifting the tent flap she saw, not blackness and nothingness as she had expected but a sky suddenly lower, closer to Rokam, a sky filled with a thousand shimmering stars, more brilliant than anything she had seen in her life before. Beautiful. Terrifying. How could so much light seem so cold?

She let the flap drop and scurried over to the cushions, wrapped herself in the softness of the quilt, and buried her head, her doll clutched in her grasp. She dozed and her legs jerked her awake. The ground seemed to sway beneath her in the trundling, ungainly gait of the kroklyn. Then, surprisingly, Atbin was shaking her awake and outside a cold dawn was breaking.

A harsh wind smoked across the surface of the gray sand and she shivered, longing for a hot drink; but all she got was a mouthful of flat water and a handful of dates. Then they were off again, riding toward the sunrise, Rania huddled for warmth among the cushions of her litter, Atbin perched on the saddle in front, singing his monotonous desert drone.

The sun rose, huge and red, painting the gray desert scarlet. Within a short time it was a blazing white disk cut out of molten steel, the wind was a gust from a baker's oven, and mirages of tossing palm trees and cool water taunted them from across the shimmering sand.

They finished their second day's journey well before sunset, in a pretty oasis green with date palms and zaramint bushes, an oasis with four wells, large drinking troughs for the animals, and a *bathhouse*.

"Oh, Atbin, may I—?"

"Of course, Princess. We'll be busy looking after the kroklyns for a while."

The bathhouse was roofed, with pillars instead of

walls so that, crouched in the cool and shaded water, Rania could see in the distance the drivers' struggle to restrain the kroklyns' furious appetite for water and could hear their screams. She let herself sink under the water in the stone cistern, her hair floating wide, and blew bubbles to the surface.

She soaked blissfully, half asleep, until Atbin's insistent murmur: "Princess, Princess," stirred her.

"All right. I'm coming!" She climbed out of the stone tank, shaking the water off her body and wringing it from her long hair. As she shook the sand from her travel-stained robe and slipped it over her wet body she suddenly giggled, remembering Nan's bathtime ritual, with perfumed oil and soap and instructions about washing behind her ears and between her toes. She looked down at her bare feet and squished her toes into the sand. It felt good.

Atbin hurried her to her tent, its door modestly open in the opposite direction, toward the desert. "Now we will bathe," he warned her.

"Don't be too long, Atbin," She told him. "I want to explore *everything*."

But she fell asleep and was wakened by voices and laughter, the smell of woodsmoke and of something delicious cooking. She scrambled out of her tent and looked around. A column of blue smoke rose steadily to the blue sky. The sun was low in the west. There was a gentle breeze. Here among the trees it was much cooler than out in the open desert.

As she walked toward the smoke something dry lightly brushed her bare toes. She looked down and froze. A snake, patterned with a brown zigzag on cream scales, wriggled across her foot. She moaned and then managed to scream through her tight throat. "Atbin!"

He was there, sand spurting from beneath his feet. "Princess, what is it?"

She pointed, her finger shaking, and his scared face broke into a relieved smile. He picked up the snake by its tail and tossed it into the bushes. "It's only a slima, Princess. Very tasty. We are roasting some for supper now."

He led her to the fire and the drivers made room for her. One of them offered her a stick with lumps of meat skewered on it.

"Slima?" she asked. They nodded, their teeth flashing in wide grins, their eyes shining in the firelight. She hesitated and then took the stick. She bit cautiously into the first piece of meat. I won't think about what it is, she told herself. She swallowed. It was tender and sweet, with a faint taste of herbs. She took another bite. "It's delicious," she said with her mouth full.

"Look out for the bones," Atbin warned her, and she picked the flesh off with her teeth and threw the bones into the fire. The drivers, who had been watching her closely, seemed to relax, and one of them spoke to the others in an accent so thick that she had to ask Atbin what he had said.

"He says that you are a true child of the desert." His dark blue eyes looked at her approvingly and she glowed inside, as if she had just been given a special present.

The third day was a repetition of the first. Peering out of her litter, Rania saw sand in every direction, broken only by stretches of hardpan clay, crazed into wide cracks so evenly patterned that it looked as if the land had been paved with huge six-sided tiles. On this clay nothing grew at all. It was a more desolate place than Rania could have imagined, on Roshan or anywhere else on Rokam. The kroklyns were restless and the drivers urged them forward, anxious to be rid of this terrible place.

It was dark before they stopped for the night and dawn when they set out again. On the afternoon of the fourth day, the landscape changed again and they began to cross a succession of wind-carved dunes.

"We call them the Restless Hills," Atbin told her.

"That's a funny name."

"They are never the same. Some people say that the spirits of travelers who have died crossing the desert inhabit them, and that's why they are always moving. The spirits within keep trying to reach their journey's end."

Rania shivered and peered through the curtains of her litter as they passed between the hills. They seemed solid enough, carved by the wind into wonderful curves, like frozen waves.

I wonder if it's a true story, she thought. After all, ghosts are possible. And this place is stranger than anything I have ever seen before, in all of Kamalant and Komilant. Soon we will be there and I must meet Sandwriter. I don't want to. She frightens me. I want to be home with Nan and Stefril. With Mother and Father. I wish none of this were happening. Perhaps if I close my eyes and wish hard enough it won't happen. It'll be a dream . . . just a dream . . . .

"See, Princess!" Atbin's voice was shrill with happiness. "Over there is the oasis of Ahman. We are *home.*"

Rania followed his pointing finger and saw the tasseled tops of palm trees silhouetted against a brassy sky. "But where's your village? I don't see anything."

He laughed. "It's underground, a big square courtyard open to the sky, with rooms in its walls carved out of the stone of Roshan. I wish you could come home and see it. I wish you could meet my mother and father and stay with us." His cheeks flushed. "Though it's very humble, compared with the palace you're used to."

"I wish I could. Perhaps Sandwriter will let me stay

with your family while I learn whatever it is I must learn."

"It's not possible, Princess. I must take you straight to Sandwriter. She will be waiting."

"Not in your village?"

"She doesn't live with *us*. No, over there." He pointed to his left and Rania pulled back the side curtains to see a dune higher than any she had seen before. Its crest reared above their heads and its shadow swallowed the ground ahead of them. "It's the Great Dune." His voice dropped to a reverent whisper.

"Look, Atbin, the other drivers are leaving us."

"They will take the southeast path to the oasis. They don't feel at ease so close. Even the shadow of the Great Dune is sacred."

Their kroklyn smelled the water in the oasis and struggled to bear right after the others. Atbin's attention was fully occupied in keeping its head over to the left, along the foot of the dune. Halfway along its great length he reined back, kicked the kroklyn to its knees, jumped down and hobbled it with a line from the bridle to its rear legs.

"Come, Princess. We have arrived. Give me your hand. We must climb."

"Up there?" She leaned back to look at the smoking crest. "Why, it's as steep as a roof."

"I'll help you. You'll be all right."

Heart thudding, eyes darkening as the blood rushed to her head, Rania plodded up the steep slope beside him, her bare feet slipping on the scorching sand. Once, near the top, they paused for breath and Atbin turned to point. "Look, you can see my home from here."

"Home" looked like a pattern of shadow-squares on the sand between the dune and the oasis. It looked like a vast castles-board, each square the courtyard of an underground house.

"I'd never been away from home before," he said shyly.

"Weren't you scared?"

"Yes, I was terrified. But it was for Sandwriter, so it was my honor and my family's honor for me to go. But I'm happy to be safely home. I hope I'll never have to cross that sea again." He took her hand and helped her up the last steep slope to the ridge.

"Oh!" Rania stared in surprise. Instead of the view of empty desert or dunes, there rose before her a great red rock, almost a mountain. It was as high as the Great Dune, so that from the crest she looked across a narrow valley directly at its peaks. The evening sun, low in the west, outlined its craggy shape and shadowed the crevices and cave mouths, so that it looked rather like an enormous red sponge rising from the brown sand.

"We must go down there." Atbin pointed at the stony valley that lay between the dune and the mountain. They skidded down the far side, digging their bare heels into the sand to slow their slide. They arrived at the bottom out of breath in a flurry of loose sand and Rania began to laugh. They she saw the expression on Atbin's face and the laughter caught in her throat.

"What is it?" She licked her dry lips.

"Don't be afraid," he said softly as she drew back. "It's all right. Come."

He led her along the narrow valley toward a column of sandstone carved in a curious shape, whether by the wind or by human hands she could not tell. He fell to his knees at its base, tugging her hand until she knelt there with him.

"What is it? What are we doing?"

"Hush. We must wait for Sandwriter here, close to the sacred handar."

"But where? She can't live *here*. You mean I'm to stay?" She looked wildly around her, at the bleak stone-strewn valley, the dune rearing above it to one side, the red cliff of the mountain to the other. To east and west it wound out of sight. In the strip of sky above a great bird circled slowly, waiting.

3

*A*tbin, you can't mean I'm to stay *here*? And where are all my belongings—my clothes, my comb and brush, my doll?"

"You will not need them, child."

Rania jumped and screamed. The voice was deep with age but not harsh, although the words themselves were.

"You must come to me as if you were newborn, naked, with nothing of the world with you. Do you understand?"

Rania looked up to see a figure as worn by time and the weather as the handar, a woman clothed in a ragged robe of homespun, the brown of the desert. *Sandwriter*. She could not answer.

"Come, child."

Numbly she took the bony, dry hand that was held out to her. She got to her feet and walked at the old woman's side away from the handar. Looking over her shoulder, hoping that perhaps, at this very moment, Atbin would say that it was all a mistake, that she was to go home and stay with his mother, go home to Malan, to Mother and Father, to Stefril and Nan, she saw him turn and begin to climb the steep slope of the dune.

Sandwriter led her along the foot of the cliff, past shadowy clefts and openings, and stopped beside one, so she was half hidden in the shadow. "Come," she said again. "Come here, child."

Rania turned once more to the dune. Atbin was at the crest now. He turned, just for an instant, and waved his hand before vanishing out of sight. Rania's hand stirred at her side, although she did not wave. She turned to look at Sandwriter. The old woman had thrown back her hood. Her hair was long and white, her eyes a brilliant blue. Roshan eyes. Father's eyes. Rania tried to return their piercing gaze without wavering.

At length Sandwriter nodded, as though satisfied at something she saw or felt. "Get out of those robes, child."

Obediently Rania stripped and stood naked on the hot sand. She felt a hand at the nape of her neck and flinched. Her heavy hair was lifted. She heard the thick sound of a knife sawing through the tresses. Her head was suddenly light. She looked down to see her long black hair lying at her feet. Her mouth fell open, though she could not say a word.

"Now put this on."

It was a simple hooded garment of scratchy brown homespun. Rania slipped it over her head and tied it with the twisted length of cord that Sandwriter handed to her.

"Follow me closely." Sandwriter turned from the sunlight and the sand and the blue sky, where the great bird still circled lazily overhead. She took a lighted torch from a holder on the wall of the cave, held it aloft and walked toward the darkness.

The cave narrowed and became a passage, apparently leading into the mountain itself. Sandwriter walked swiftly, the light going with her, so that Rania had no choice but to follow close behind, despite her fear. The walls of the passage seemed to close around her. She could feel the whole weight of the mountain over her head. Their bare feet were so silent on the rocky floor that she could hear the small creaks and sighs and the distant dripping of water that was the mountain talking to itself. Terrified, Rania clutched the rough cloth of Sandwriter's robe.

Their way seemed to twist and turn. There were side passages branching to right and left. The old woman's feet moved surely over rough rock and across narrow stone bridges beneath which was only darkness. They seemed to be going down and down into the very heart of Rokam itself. Then, when Rania's terror was almost unbearable, the path began to rise again. Soon it was quite steep; a little later it was carved into steps.

Slowly Rania became aware of light ahead. She could see the gray roughness of the walls beyond the small golden flicker of torchlight. The passage suddenly widened into an airy cave, floored with clean sand. There was an arched opening in front of her, through which Rania could see the desert stretching, unbroken by dunes or rocks, to the northern horizon. Sunset glowed redly over to her left. They had walked right through the mountain!

Stefril would never believe me if I told him I had walked through a mountain, she thought, and bit her lip to stop herself from crying. Will I ever seen Stefril again?

She turned from the cave mouth to look at the cave itself. Was *this* to be her home? There were two mattresses, each made of the same scratchy homespun as their robes, each with a small pillow and a hairy brown blanket. On the back of the left wall a sooty stain showed where the fire must be made. A few unadorned clay dishes and a metal cooking pot stood neatly in a niche in the rock. Close to the entrance of the cave was a small plain mat.

Was this Sandwriter's home? Was this really the sum total of her possessions? And was this to be *her* home also? The memory of her own pretty gray and white room jumped into her mind: the bed mounded with cushions, the soft drapes blowing at the window, the cool marble floor, the safety of Mother's and Father's room on the one side, the nursery on the other. Dear fat Nan. She would give anything to hear Nan complaining about her back and her fallen arches and naughty children once more. And Stefril—

She swallowed and turned from her inspection of the cave to find Sandwriter's gaze upon her. Once more she tried to meet the piercing eyes without blinking or lowering her own. After all, she *was* a princess and heir to the throne of Kamalant and Komilant. Her chin went up.

Sandwriter stooped to light a small bright fire of thorn twigs and set upon it a potful of water and chopped vegetables. She turned and squatted without a word on the small mat that lay at the cave mouth.

Silence. Like a skein of thread, it wound around Rania and pulled her slowly forward until she too was at the cave entrance. The mountain sloped downward to meet the northern desert which lay, perhaps the height of a house, below them. She felt awkward standing alone, so after a while she too squatted on the mat beside Sandwriter.

The silence wound in tighter and tighter. The silence of the desert and the sky. Of the vast spaces.

She felt as imprisoned in silence as a bird wrapped in clay before being baked in the oven. She could hear the thudding of her heart and the singing of the blood in her ears growing louder and louder until it was deafening.

When the last vestige of light had gone from the sky Sandwriter went back into the cave, stirred the fire, and ladled out two bowls of vegetable broth. Sitting in silence, side by side on the mat, the two drank their soup and ate a single slice of flatbread.

Still without a word Sandwriter showed Rania which bed was hers. She lay on the lumpy mattress under the harsh blanket with her eyes wide open. The fire died out and now the cave was black, the only light coming through its entrance from a sky brimming over with stars, more stars than there were grains of sand in the desert below.

She lay watching the star patterns cross the sky from east to west as Rokam turned. She could feel beneath her the stone sphere that *was* Rokam. She could feel it move among the stars in its part of the Great Dance of the Sky. She was as small as a grain of sand. She was nothing. But, borne upon the back of the planet, she too was part of the Dance.

Atbin turned at the crest of the Great Dune to look back. He knew he should not; Sandwriter was to be seen only when she chose and certainly not looked down upon. Her back was toward him. Beside her the little princess looked very small and lonely. He waved and saw her face, as white as her robe, framed in the black silky hair that fell over her shoulders. He thought he saw her hand tremble and begin to lift, like a caged bird, before he turned again to run down the far side of the dune toward his impatient kroklyn.

The evening sun was staining the sandstone steps pinky red when he raced down the stairs into the shadow of the underground courtyard that was the center of the house. It was empty. Pots bubbled on the glowing cook-fire.

"Mother, Father! It's me, Atbin!"

Out of the open doorways they came running, parents, aunts, uncles, cousins.

"Atbin! We saw the caravan and hoped it was yours. How are you?" His father grasped his hand.

Then his mother exclaimed that he had grown at least a handspan in the three ten-days he had been gone. His cousins crowded around, tugging at his travel robe for attention. The uncles lit the lamps, even though the sun had not yet set, and hung them from the branches of the big fig tree in the middle of the courtyard. Stew was spooned by the aunts into gourd dishes and loaves of flatbread were piled on the table.

Between mouthfuls Atbin tried to answer their questions. "The sea? Yes, it's even wider than the desert. We sailed for eight days, day and night, before we saw land. A ship isn't like a kroklyn. It doesn't have to eat or sleep, but sails on and on without stopping."

"Imagine that! Tell us about Malan. Is it as big as . . . as Lohat?"

"As big? Why, you could put Lohat into Malan ten times over! And the houses are very large and made of stone, all colors, white and green and swirling colors, as smooth as—I can't tell you how smooth. But the strangest thing was the palace—"

"Think of our Atbin in the great palace of Malan!"

"Hush, stop gabbing and listen to the boy."

"In the center of the main courtyard is a big pool of water and in the middle of it a thing called a 'fountain,' which sends water spouting up into the air in jets of different heights. Some of it blows away in spray and the rest runs down into the basin. And this fountain goes day and night."

"Is it for washing in? For doing the laundry?"

Atbin shook his head, tore off a piece of bread and stuffed it into his mouth. "No, it's not used for anything," he mumbled.

"But it must be for something. Perhaps it's a secret. They didn't tell you."

"No. It's to look at. To be refreshing."

"Imagine all that water running away. Wasting."

"There was a storm one night, so I went out and stood naked in the blessed rain. A palace guard ran up to me and told me to get dressed again. It's very unpleasant to be in the rain in wet clothes. They let the water run about everywhere."

"There were no rain barrels? No cisterns?"

"None that I could see." Atbin wolfed another piece of bread.

"So it seems the stories about the rain gods favoring the twin continents are true after all," exclaimed one of Atbin's cousins.

An old aunt smacked his ear. "Of course they're true."

"What did the princess look like?"

"Well, she's no taller than you, thin and pale with dark straight hair."

"She sounds very ugly."

"No—not ugly. Different. Her dress for the birthday was very grand. Embroidered all over with jewels."

"Really? What else?"

"I don't remember any more. Mother, she looked so small down in the sacred valley. Alone with *her* for the rest of her life."

Shudi's hand flew up in a make-good gesture. "You're not questioning *her* ways, I hope, my son. What strange habits have you picked up in Kamalant?"

"No one in Kamalant ever speaks of Sandwriter, Mother. I don't think they know who she is. When I spoke her name to the guard he laughed at me and wouldn't let me pass. Only the queen and the young chief understood the meaning of her gift. Perhaps it's only in Roshan that—"

"Hush!" Shudi put her hand over her son's mouth. "She holds the safety of all Rokam in her hands. Every sensible person knows that."

"Yes, Mother, I didn't mean—" Atbin gave a jaw-cracking yawn. "There was meat at every meal, Mother, and sauces and sweet things such as you've never tasted before. But there's nothing as satisfying as your bread. I used to dream of it. It's good to be home."

"Flatterer!" Shudi struck his shoulder. "Go to bed. Get on with you. You're asleep on your feet."

He stumbled obediently into the room carved out of sandstone that lay behind the one where his mother and father slept. He pulled off his desert robe, rolled onto his sleeping shelf and pulled a homespun blanket up to his waist. He did not stir until the sun was high next day.

When he went into the courtyard, blinking in the bright sun and scratching himself lazily, he found his mother preparing the daily basket of vegetables, bread, and fruit that was the village offering to Sandwriter.

"You'll have to put more in, now the princess is living with *her*."

"Trying to teach your mother to catch slima, are you? Since you know so much, tell me what I am supposed to do with this." She pointed to the bundle that Atbin had unloaded from the kroklyn the evening before.

"It is to go back to Lohat, I suppose. The tent and rug, the cushions and dishes, they all belong to the lady Sufi."

"Tchah! How badly you have bundled it up. It's all crumpled. Look at this cloth, did you ever see weaving so fine?" Her rough hands smoothed the fabric. "But these are not the lady Sufi's. Here is the princess's toilet box and her doll. Oh, Atbin, how careless of you. The child will be lonely without her doll, a favorite, I'll be bound. I'll slip it into the basket with the food."

He put his hand over hers. "No, Mother. The princess was to go to Sandwriter with nothing of her own, nothing at all."

Shudi's lips tightened, but she said nothing. She wrapped the doll carefully in a cloth and tucked it into the bigger bundle along with the toilet box.

"If the basket of food is ready, perhaps I can take it."

"See the hunting spider strut! Your visit to Kamalant has swelled your head, Atbin. You know full well that it is your father's privilege, as headman of the village, to deliver the basket to Sandwriter every day, as it is *my* privilege to prepare it."

"Yes, Mother."

"But you can take it up to him."

"Yes, Mother." Atbin took the basket and bounded up the stairs to the desert floor.

Why do I want to see her again? he asked himself. She is only a skinny little girl, after all, even if she *is* a princess. But he could not wipe from his mind that last picture of her standing below him in a sacred valley, so small in her white robe, her hand fluttering at her side.

When Atmon returned from delivering the basket that afternoon, carrying yesterday's empty basket, he brought with him also a white robe. "It was lying on the ground, close to the handar," he reported. "And there were locks of black hair. Long black hair."

"Now she has nothing at all of her own," said Atbin, touching the robe.

"What must be, must be," snapped Shudi. She shook out the robe, the last remnant of the princess Rania, folded it neatly, and tucked it into the bundle to be returned to Lohat. Seven days later a caravan from Monar rested overnight in the oasis of Ahman. When it left for Lohat the following morning, the bundle went with it.

Should I go back to the sacred valley and take some of her hair, just as a memento? Atbin asked himself. But it was a foolish idea, after all, and wrong. He had no business in the valley.

Atmon kept him hard at work planting beans, and slowly the memory of his journey to fabulous Kamalant faded. After the beans flowered and began to fruit, it was time to prepare for the tenth birthday of one of Atbin's cousins. There was a bustle of cooking and making of gifts, for the whole village would share in the rejoicing.

Atbin searched the desert until he found a piece of thornwood already twisted into almost the shape he wanted. He carved it into the likeness of a doll and persuaded his mother to fashion a dress for it out of a scrap of leftover cloth.

When he saw how his ten-year-old cousin held his gift in her arms, and the expression of happiness on her face, the last memory of the princess Rania came back to him with startling clarity. *Her* arms were empty. *She* had nothing to hold.

He could not get this picture out of his mind. He began to search for another piece of thornwood. When at last he found it, he began to carve it secretly into the likeness of another doll. He stole a patch from his mother's workbox and fashioned a rough dress for it, cutting a hole for the head and tying it about the waist with a piece of twine.

When it was finished he hid it under a stone at the back of his sleeping room. It might be years before he would have permission to cross the Great Dune and set foot in the sacred valley. But when that time comes, he promised himself, the princess will have her doll.

4

*R*ania woke, shivering, and groped for her doll. It must have fallen out of bed. And the covers . . . . She opened her eyes and stared in bewilderment at the rock ceiling and then, remembering, at the motionless figure framed in the entrance of the cave. Had Sandwriter slept at all?

She got out of bed, shivering, and groped for her robe in the half-dark. "Good morning," she said politely to the silent figure. There was no answer. She stood uncertainly and then went to sit on the mat next to the old woman.

Sandwriter's hood was thrown back and her white hair shone in the pearly light. Her sunken eyes stared blindly out at . . . at what? There was nothing to see out there but the brown desert, as flat as the sea, stretching to the northern horizon.

After a long boring time in which Rania sat, staring at her hands and playing nursery finger-games, like castle roofs and staircases, the sun suddenly rose in a splendor of color. The sand became golden-brown, the cave filled with light, and Sandwriter moved, stretched, and got to her feet.

Still without saying a word, she took from the food basket a disk of flatbread and a handful of dates and figs. She broke the bread in two, halved the fruit and handed one share to Rania. Rania swallowed the food in gulps, feeling that she'd never been so hungry in her life.

"Please, what else is there? I'm still starving."

Sandwriter peered at her as if she were seeing her for the first time, and then handed her more bread and fruit. It was not until she had licked the last drop of purple juice from her fingers that Rania realized that Sandwriter was not eating, that she had taken *her* food. I'll never do that again, she told herself. How awful! She learned this first lesson without the old woman saying a word.

That silent lesson set a pattern for the days that followed. Each day Sandwriter and Rania rose before dawn to sit cross-legged at the cave mouth, waiting to greet the rising sun. Afterward they broke their fast with flatbread, fruit, and cold water. Then they walked, leaving the cave by the northern entrance, which sloped gently down to the desert floor. When Rania looked back, all she could see was the red mountain and, occasionally, the high crest of the Great Dune beyond. They never returned through the secret passages to the sacred valley or went south past the Great Dune to the village where Atbin and his family lived.

She thought about him often, when she and Sandwriter rested in the cool cave in the heat of the afternoon. What would he be doing? What was his mother like? Did he remember her? Probably not. He would have a busy life planting things, looking after the kroklyns, whatever it was that desert farmers did.

It was during the late afternoon, following more lessons, that Sandwriter would disappear into the darkness of the passage at the back of the cave, to return some time later with the basket containing the next day's food. If I could only put a note in it, thought Rania desperately, to tell them how hungry I am—but it was impossible, of course. She often thought of the journey from Lohat and how she had refused to eat more than a bite of the delicate gazelle meat that Atbin had begged her to finish. If she only had that meat now! Sometimes when Sandwriter returned with the basket, it was all that Rania could do not to snatch it out of her hands and gobble the contents.

But there was still another lesson of sorts and a meditation as they watched the sun set, before she could eat again and go to sleep, curled up around her emptiness and loneliness. Mother and Father, Stefril and Nan, were so far away that even imagining talking to them was impossible. But Atbin, who had been so kind and gentle to her, lived only beyond the mountain and the dune. No great distance. He could visit her and be home in almost no time at all. If *only* he would.

He never did, of course. Why should he? She was only a ten-year-old child, forgotten by the world. Outside the cave was only the desert. When the wind blew hard, columns of sand and clouds of dust moved across its face. The dunes, like restless giants, moved forward, back, around, forming new ridges, fans, stars.

Only the Great Dune, perhaps anchored by the presence of the mountain, or by the greater magic of Sandwriter, never moved, even though the wind blew the sand continuously from its crest.

"Perhaps the Great Dune is like me," she said to Sandwriter one day. "My skin sheds, my fingernails grow. I am changing all the time. But I am still *me*."

Sandwriter nodded. Rania had become used to the fact that she seldom spoke, and sometimes she wondered if she too might actually forget words, through using them so seldom. When she was alone Rania talked aloud all the time so that this would not happen to her.

Occasionally on their daily walks Sandwriter

would say a few words. Rania had thought at first that this was playtime, but she soon learned that there was no such thing as play, that every moment of the day was some kind of learning.

"Go back to the cave," Sandwriter told her one day, as she ran from dune to dune. "Fetch me a drink of water."

Rania looked around. The red mountain was, for the moment, out of sight behind the dunes. No matter. I can follow my footprints back, she thought, and set out, retracing her dancing footprints back and around, up one small dune and down another. The footprints became fainter and fainter, until she came to a place where the wind had scrubbed the sand clean.

I'm lost, she thought, and turned to retrace her steps. But the constant wind wiped out the footsteps she had just made as well. She stopped on the sand, trapped in the small space between the past and future, the wind erasing her steps up to where she stood.

It was almost noon. There were no clear shadows pointing south or north. Only the sun overhead, its heat drying her body. She could not see Sandwriter. There was nothing familiar.

"I won't be beaten," she said aloud and began to walk briskly in the direction that felt right. Then Sandwriter's hands were on her shoulders, turning her around.

"In two ten-days or so, if you had not died of thirst, you would be back in Lohat. *This* is the way."

"How do you know?"

"See how the sand lies. The steady winds come out of the southeast, except during the great storms. The desert is shaped by the hand of the wind. See the sharp slope of this dune and the slow slope. Now show me where east is."

Rania pointed.

"Now notice the plants, how they grow in groups, though spaced far apart from each other. Look at the pattern. See where the roots reach down for water. There is enough for each plant, because they are not greedy. And the water paths lead back to the sacred mountain."

"Is that why it is sacred?" Rania asked, but Sandwriter seemed not to have heard.

Some of the lessons were silent ones. They squatted for hours in the sun beside a funnel-shaped hole, a tiny spot only noticeable because the cast-out grains of sand made a faint fan shape to the south of the hole. Finally a tiny reddish sand beetle appeared, its antenna waving, and scurried eagerly toward the fan. It began to slide down the funnel and tried to scramble back. The more it struggled, the faster it slid until it vanished down the hole.

Rania moved and Sandwriter put a hand on her arm. They waited. The sweat trickled down Rania's forehead. After a time a feather-leg whisked out of the hole and smoothed the disturbed sand into a fresh fan shape.

"Why *did* the beetle fall in?" Rania asked. "And why was it so silly as to pick this one place to walk?"

Sandwriter didn't answer and Rania crouched over the hole, working it out for herself. "The sand must be different here and that's why I can spot the fan-shape from a long way off." She picked up a few grains and rolled them across the palm of her hand. "They're coated with something to make them round and smooth."

She touched the grains in her hand with her tongue. They were as sweet as honey. No wonder the beetle had come. The trap was no longer a mystery and the desert had revealed one of its secrets to her. I won, she thought triumphantly. One day I shall know *everything*.

On the walk back to the cave her mouth began to burn. By the time they reached it there was a blister on her tongue and her mouth felt as if it were on fire. Sandwriter brewed a bitter lotion to rinse out her mouth with, but she couldn't eat for two days. That was the end of the lesson. But still Sandwriter didn't say a word.

In the heat of afternoon, lessons took place in the cave. These were more boring than anything that had ever happened to Rania before. She had to sit perfectly still and gaze into the flames of a small fire built in the cave entrance, or look into a dish of water or, worst of all, sit cross-legged, staring out across the desert, a handful of sand in each outstretched hand.

After these lessons Rania felt like a jug that had been emptied and left out in the sun, so that there was not a single drop of self left in her. She felt dry and empty, longing to be filled with something: but what? Sandwriter would never tell her.

Then, one afternoon, everything changed. She was staring, as usual, into the heart of the fire. It seemed that the red embers gathered together into a ball of fire that pulsed and grew. She gasped out loud and the light broke apart like a shattered pot.

"What did you see, child?"

When Rania tried to explain, Sandwriter nodded. "You have seen the creation. The beginning."

Rania's heart pounded, because something in the old woman's voice told her that *now* her real education was about to begin, that the past learning had been nothing but a preparation, as the farmer plows his field before planting the seed.

"In the beginning," Sandwriter said, in her deep old voice, "Rokam was a ball of fire. Little by little it cooled. Then the rain began to fall and the molten rocks cracked, just as a pot does if you put too hot a liquid in it. One great crack ran from north to south and separated the island of Roshan from the continent of Kamalant-Komilant. Slowly they too were pulled apart, until only an isthmus held the twin continents together.

"Slowly the lands drifted apart, so that now the Small Sea separates us from Kamalant and Komilant. As the lands separated, so did the people, even though they had once been brothers. They began to think only of themselves, rather than the good of all peoples and of Rokam. But that is another story. . . ."

After a time Rania said, "A housewife would throw away a cracked pot and buy another from the potter."

Silence.

"Only I suppose you cannot throw away a broken world and start over."

Silence.

"Perhaps it would be better to try and mend it. But how? After all, the world is not really like a pot."

The silence went on for a long time. Rania gazed into the fire. The last flame had found a vein of resin in a twig and danced along it, green and blue light.

"You are the housewife," Rania discovered. "*You* are the glue and *yours* are the hands that hold the pot together until the glue dries. That is what you *are*."

Sandwriter got to her feet and went to chop the vegetables for their evening's soup. From that day on, Rania was made to work even harder, until she could find her way anywhere in the desert, tell the presence of water, not only by plants, but by the prickling in her thumbs; she could tell the hour of the night and the season of the year by the stars; she could keep the picture of a map in her head and repeat, word for word, every story Sandwriter told her.

"But it is only through endurance that the power over sand and wind can come," Sandwriter said when she moaned that she was too tired to go on.

Power. Rania remembered the gruesome story Nan had told her, of the traitor Eskoril and how Sandwriter had killed him through wind and sand. She shivered. "Will I learn this power?" she asked, half wanting to, half afraid.

"The secret power of Roshan is not in the wind or the sand. It is in understanding and quietness." She picked up the torch that hung by the passage at the back of the cave and lit it. "Come, child."

Now, for the first time, Rania followed Sandwriter back into the dark passage through which she had come so long before. How long? How many tendays? How many years? All this time, the two of us alone. It is incredible, she thought. How have I endured it?

Her heart pounded as she followed the light and the homespun brown robe ahead of her. Perhaps we will go back to the valley. Perhaps we will visit the village and see Atbin and meet his family. To talk to another human being— Her arms stretched out in front of her, yearning, but Sandwriter appeared not to see.

She turned into a passage that led down steep steps, the torch flickering over the grotesque knobs and protuberances on the passage walls and roof. As the light moved over them they took on human or beastly form, so that as they walked faces leapt out at them, leering, snarling, then falling back into darkness as a new gallery of gargoyles sprang to life.

I would have remembered *this*, Rania thought. So we are not going to the valley after all. This is another lesson.

It grew uncomfortably hot. Gusts of air from cracks in the walls brought strange odors. The mountain itself creaked and whispered, as if commenting on these strangers who walked through its secret ways. Rania swallowed the fear that mounted inside her, but it seemed that they had been walking for an eternity before Sandwriter's pace slackened.

"Take my hand and close your eyes," she ordered.

Rania obeyed her and they walked slowly on.

"What do you feel now?"

"Space. Coolness. Damp."

Sandwriter seemed to wait.

Rania listened. A faint musical note came to her ears. It came again and with it a faint echo. And again.

"Water falling into water."

Still Sandwriter waited.

"Peace," said Rania at last.

"Open your eyes."

She obeyed and cried out, and her cry was echoed again and again from the walls of the vast cave in which they stood. The light of the single torch was reflected off pillars and buttresses, swags and draperies, all decked out in jewel-bright flashes of red and blue, gold and green. It was like being in a giant's throne room that was draped, not in embroidered silk, but in stone.

"Oh!" She turned round and round, rejoicing in the splendor, until her eye was suddenly caught by the one still place that lay, like a dark eye, at the center.

It was a pool of water, so deep as to be black, shadowed from the brilliance around it. Every once in a while a single drop of water would fall from one of the stone hangings above. As it hit the water rings of movement shivered out to the edges of the pool. The water would quiver and become still. Until the next drop fell. Rania felt that she could watch it forever.

"You may drink, child."

She walked slowly forward and cupped her hands in the water. It was cold, pure, and sweet, drawn from the very heart of Roshan. She felt that if she could bathe here, she would never be tired or thirsty again.

"This is the secret heart of Roshan. This is the place where the rain gods hid the water for which our ancestor Calman prayed in the beginning times, after his greedy brothers of Kamalant and Komilant had stolen all the rain."

"It is not just a story? It really happened?"

"What is story? What is happening? Now I will

teach you the secret ways of the mountain. You must learn them well, so that you will never mistake the lie for the truth, the false passage for the real. But until you have learned every twist and turn, every division of the ways, you must not come here alone."

"I will learn them, I will!"

From that day every spare moment was spent in learning the mountain paths.

"Who built them?" Rania asked, shrinking back one day from a pit that opened into darkness before her feet.

"No person. The mountain made its own paths and its own way of protecting them in the beginning, when the hot rock ran about inside Rokam and the water ate away at the rock. But the stairs have been carved by hand, long before my time, long before the time of her who came before me."

For how many turns of Rokam had different Sand-writers trodden these dark paths? Rania wondered. And how many apprentices before her had learned the secret ways?

There were, in fact, only two main passages, each running through the mountain from south to north. There was the one through which she had come from the valley in the south to the cave in which she and Sandwriter lived on the north face of the mountain.

The second also had its beginning in the valley below the Great Dune, but it was a more subtle and dangerous way, marked with false divisions, dead ends and traps. At its halfway point beneath the mountain lay the pool in the cave of light. In the cave wall, if one knew where to look, was another narrow path leading downward into what Rania thought of as the dark mystery.

This pool, too, was dark, but filled with an evil liquid far different from water. When Sandwriter touched her torch to it, the surface of the water broke into devilish flames.

"It is like the difference between good and evil. How strange that the mountain should hold them both."

"No stranger than finding the same two in the heart of every human being," Sandwriter had replied.

On the northern side of the dark cave was a narrow staircase, which led up and up to emerge on a ledge dizzily high above the desert on the northern face of the mountain. When Rania looked cautiously over the edge she thought she could see, far below, to the right, the entrance to *their* cave.

One passage connected the direct route through the mountain with the cave of light and therefore with the other passage, so that it was possible to go from north to south directly or in a kind of x pattern.

Once Rania had learned every twist and turn of every passage, false and true, she was allowed to spend part of her afternoons meditating in the pool of light. The quietness, the rhythmic dripping of water, was like the rhythm of her own body. After a while, it began to seem to her like a clock, telling away the days and years of her life, the untold time she had spent with Sandwriter. She could feel the past slipping away and, afraid, she reached out to it, deliberately making herself recall her first meeting with Sandwriter; Atbin and his kindness on their journey across Roshan. Then back, back to Malan. To Father and Mother. Nan and Stefril. Back to the memory of the wind in her hair and the sense of being like a bird as she rode the caramel-colored pony, Freedom. He had been hers for only a day. Less really. He had only truly been hers until the moment Sandwriter reached out across the sea and claimed her with the box of sand.

5

*O*nce the beans were picked and the vines bundled for kroklyn feed, Atbin helped his father repair the cisterns in the oasis. When that pleasantly cool job was completed, it was time to plant and then harvest another crop of beans, before tropical winter turned into the burning agony of tropical summer. The land cracked. The wind blew out of a furnace. The people stayed underground and endured.

The sun swung northward again and the rains came, a few precious storms whose waters were led down the slopes, along paths laid with carefully chosen pebbles, into covered conduits. The young people danced naked in the rain and the old ones sang the thanksgiving songs.

Then, once more, as in the old story, the rain gods turned their backs on Roshan, and other drought was endured. Another rain. Another drought, as Rokam turned.

Atmon struggled with his newly purchased kroklyn. It had cost twenty armspans of Shudi's best hand-woven cloth in the market at Monar, five days' riding to the north, and it had seemed a good bargain at the time. Now he was not so sure.

He hammered a spike into the hard ground, caught the bridle rope, and hitched it securely to the spike. The kroklyn jerked its head uneasily and Atmon hit it behind its knees until the beast grunted and knelt. Atmon approached it cautiously from behind its left flank. The wedge-shaped head whipped around, the teeth gleaming, greenish saliva dripping to the sand. Atmon leapt out of harm's way. The line held and the kroklyn's head was jerked to a halt.

"Take care, Father. I don't trust the look of that beast. Let me help."

"Keep out of my way, Atbin. I've been breaking kroklyns since before you were born. I know what I'm about."

Atbin sighed and chewed his lip. It wasn't right. Twenty years old, and still his father treated him like a beardless boy. He stood back as Atmon leapt for the saddle, grasped the horn and caught the reins. His left heel kicked the kroklyn's flank and the beast heaved itself to its feet with a forward and backward lurch and tried to bolt for the northern desert and Monar.

The tether rope held firm and the kroklyn was forced to run in a circle around the spike, while Atmon clung to the saddle, the reins held short in heavily gloved hands. Atbin watched with grudging admiration. His father was as obstinate as a—as a kroklyn. He would have bet his only copper coin that the kroklyn would never have allowed him to mount it. Now, as the beast bucked around the tetherspike, he guessed that Atmon was recalling with every jolt how many days it had taken Shudi to weave the cloth he had exchanged for this bad-humored beast.

Atmon seemed to have the kroklyn under control and it trotted meekly around the tetherspike, its padded feet kicking up a cloud of sand. Its tongue hung loosely between its jaws. It looked exhausted.

"Father, watch out!" Atbin called, seeing a red flash in the beast's eye that was neither meek nor exhausted. As he yelled its head came up with a violent jerk that tossed Atmon back in his saddle and broke the rope with a crack that echoed back from the Great Dune. Then it was off toward the north, toward Monar, neck outstretched, Atmon still clinging obstinately to the saddle.

Atbin leapt for the nearest grazing kroklyn. He flung a saddle over the high back, clinched the belly strap tight and slapped it behind the knees. It knelt obediently and he scrambled into the saddle. He forced it to its feet and flicked it under the belly with the loose end of the rein. "Come on, tortoise! Move!"

Atmon was already out of sight past the eastward edge of the Great Dune as Atbin urged his kroklyn to a better speed. Now he too was past the trailing edge of the dune. If it were not for the curve of Rokam itself he would be able to see Monar, five days' riding away. There was nothing but flat desert and the one small shape of the fleeing kroklyn.

Three days to the next oasis, Atbin thought. "What a fool I am," he said aloud. "I never told the others. I never stopped to bring water."

Almost he turned back but changed his mind. His father had no water either. If he was not able to stop his kroklyn soon, or if Atbin was unable to catch him, they would die of thirst anyway. He settled himself in the saddle and concentrated on shortening the distance between his mount and the small dust cloud ahead that marked the passage of the other kroklyn. The sun beat down on his shoulders and he drew his hood forward over his head.

All that morning Sandwriter had sniffed the wind, her keen eyes scanning the horizon, her gnarled hands opening and closing like the claws of a desert eagle.

"What is it? What's the matter?"

"I do not know yet. Hush, child, let me listen."

She squatted on the mat at the cave door and Rania obediently sat beside her. Outside the shadowy cave the sun beat down whitely on the blazing sand. Nothing moved but the shimmer of mirage, promising pools of water where there were none.

"Listen!" Sandwriter's hand came up as Rania cried, "Look!"

"A solitary kroklyn. One man. No provisions."

"But he's heading for Monar. That's five days away, you told me. Something must be terribly wrong. Oh, help him, please!"

Rania clutched Sandwriter's arm as she spoke. A thrill like the nearness of a lightning strike ran through her arm and her hand dropped to her side, numb.

"Do not touch me, child." Sandwriter rose to her feet and walked the few steps forward until she was standing just outside the cave, the full force of the sun beating down upon her.

Crouched on the mat, Rania looked past her at the small cloud of dust. It grew smaller and smaller. Soon it would be out of sight and the journey would be over for the luckless man on the beast's back. But now, from the right, another kroklyn appeared, striding after the first.

Rania gasped and her hand went to her mouth. It would never catch up. It was too far behind and the first beast ran as if the wind were in its feet.

The *wind*? She raised her face and felt a breath stir

her hair and cool her sweaty forehead. Then a gust. A wind, at this time of year? Out of the *north*? It was impossible.

She looked up at Sandwriter and her question dried in her mouth. The normally bent woman had become tall and straight. Her arms were stretched high above her head and from her fingertips blue fire crackled. The sky was no longer blue to the horizon. A dark band of rain-laden cloud was bearing down on them from the north, moving on the relentless wind.

Sandwriter's robe was plastered against her body and her white hair flew out behind her, but she never moved. Now the rain cloud was above the bolting kroklyn. Rain streaked black from cloud to sand. Was the maddened kroklyn slowing down at the smell and taste of rain? The distance between the two kroklyns was beginning to close. Could the second one get there in time, or would it too slow down at the scent of rain?

Lightning cracked and for an instant she was blinded. Thunder shook the sky and she saw the kroklyn rear, throw its rider and bolt for Monar. The wind dropped and in the sudden silence Rania heard a faint sigh. She jumped to her feet in time to catch the frail body of Sandwriter.

How small she is and how thin, thought Rania, as she laid the old woman carefully on her mattress. I can feel every bone. Suppose she is dead. Then there will be no Sandwriter in Roshan. Who would keep Rokam on its course then? In panic she fumbled for the thin wrist. But all was well. Her anxious fingers felt a thready flutter between the tendons.

She smoothed the white hair back from the high forehead. Sandwriter's eyelids were closed over her sunken eyes. She looked very old.

"Don't die," Rania begged her. "Please don't die. I know nothing yet. I'm not fit. And I don't want to be. I don't want to have to do . . ." She stumbled over the image of the old woman, drawn erect like a tall candle flame, lightning crackling from her fingertips.

Crouched over the still body of the old woman, Rania glanced out of the cave door. It was as if the storm had never happened. The sky was a still, piercing blue. The sand stretched to the northern horizon, its emptiness broken only by the dark shape of a kroklyn. It drew slowly nearer, until she could distinguish the shape of a robed figure in the saddle, another lying across the kroklyn's shoulders. It vanished out of sight around the east of the red mountain.

Rania turned back to Sandwriter. She wrung a cloth out in cool water and bathed her face. "Don't die," she whispered. "Please don't die."

"That broken leg will take three ten-days to heal, and how are we to manage without our headman?" Shudi scolded. "Such foolishness."

"Hush, woman. The kroklyn—"

"—was a poor choice, Atmon, admit it. I know why you kept trying to break it, but don't you understand, you silly man, that you're worth more to me than a hundred spans of cloth? Not to mention the village being without its headman for three ten-days!"

It was one of the longest speeches Atbin had ever heard his mother make. "Don't worry, Mother. I'll do Father's work. After all, I am a man, though I've had little enough chance to show it till now, haven't I, Father?"

"True enough, boy." Atmon managed a wry smile. "To be a headman's son is to grow up in the shade. Until this leg heals you'll be in the light. Let's see how you do. You'll be in charge of the village's use of water and of the crops. You'll have to look after my kroklyns too, of course, and take the daily food offering to Sandwriter. As for the rest, you must tell me everything that goes on. I can settle any village squabbles as well from my bed as from the courtyard."

"Well and good. That's settled," said Shudi briskly. "Now you will neither talk nor settle village affairs. Drink this tea to lessen the pain and sleep, husband. Come, Atbin, leave him to his rest."

She swept Atbin out of the room ahead of her, but once outside in the sunshine of the courtyard, she put her arms around his neck. "Oh, how tall you have grown! I can hardly reach. You saved his life, my son. I thank you for it."

"It was little enough I did, Mother. I didn't wait to fetch water, so I was ill prepared for a long chase. If it hadn't been for the rain squall I would never have caught up with him."

"A *rain squall*?" Shudi looked up at the dazzling sky.

"Truly, Mother. It came out of nowhere and vanished into nowhere. I've never seen anything like it. The kroklyn slowed down to drink. I believe I still wouldn't have caught up to it, but there was a single flash of lightning and it reared up and threw Father. Then it was off to the north and the rain cloud vanished."

Shudi's hands went to her mouth. "It must have been *her* doing. May she be blessed."

"You mean—?"

"Who else has power over wind and rain? She saved my man. I must find something special to put into today's food offering." She looked up at the sun and began to scurry about, choosing the choicest fruit and vegetables and packing them with three loaves of fresh flatbread into the offering basket. "Take it quickly, Atbin. All this fuss with your father put it right out of my head. Remember, leave the basket close to the handar and pick up yesterday's basket, which should be left there. And leave at once. You mustn't stay and look on Sandwriter unless she—"

"Mother, I know. You mustn't worry. Father's leg will heal fast. Until then I'll manage. I'll ask Uncle Tobin to help me."

"Yes, that would be a good thing to do. Now off with you. It's getting late."

Atbin ran up the stairs and saddled up a kroklyn. At last he was going to have the chance to show his father what he could do. He rode happily across to the Great Dune and scrambled up to the crest and down the other side. Only the solemnity of the still valley and the lowering presence of the sacred mountain wiped the grin off his face. He walked slowly, head bent, to the handar and knelt to place the basket of food at its foot.

As he picked up the empty basket lying there, the evening shadows outlined a single footprint in the sand. It was small and neatly made, a girl's or a young woman's. He sat back on his heels, suddenly remembering the day, four years ago, when he had last seen the princess Rania. She had been so little and lonely looking, standing white-faced beside the imposing Sandwriter, her black hair down her back. He could still remember the tiny movement of her hand with which she had answered his good-bye wave. The memory hurt him as much today as it had then. He bent down and laid his hand over the footprint. How small it was. Then he got to his feet and walked slowly up the slope of the Great Dune, the empty basket in his hand.

That night, lying looking at the flickering oil lamp, he wondered what the last four years must have been like for the lonely child. She had been ten then, so she must be fourteen now. Never a friend to talk to. Never a toy to play with. She had gone with nothing, he remembered, not even her long black hair.

He got up and moved a stone at the back of his room that hid a crack in which he had always kept his secret treasures. He put his hand in, felt around and drew out the doll. He turned it over in his hand, thinking what a poor thing it was and how much better he could make it now. She would probably laugh at it. At fourteen the village girls were ready for marriage and thinking about babies of their own, not dolls. But of course the apprentice of Sandwriter wouldn't be thinking of a husband, or of babies.

The following day, while Shudi prepared the fresh offering for Sandwriter, he ran back into his room and hid the doll in his robe. Once in the valley, he placed the basket of food by the handar and set the little doll on top of it. He took the empty basket and scrambled up the side of the dune, his cheeks hot at his own foolishness. At the crest he almost turned back. It was such a poor gift for a princess.

By late afternoon Sandwriter's swoon had turned into a healthy sleep. Only then did Rania realize how hungry she was. And there was nothing to eat. She looked in dismay at the empty basket and at the sleeping woman. Then she took the basket in one hand and a lit torch in the other and set out through the mountain passages toward the cave in the valley through which she had come so long ago.

"It's lucky that she taught me all the ways, or we would starve to death," she said out loud. "I must just be sure to make no mistake. Knowing in one's head is not quite the same as doing it."

Carefully she traced the route marked in her memory, turning here, avoiding a pitfull there until, triumphantly, she emerged in the narrow cave opening into the valley. The sun was beginning to cast long shadows down the valley, though it still shone on the Great Dune that reared, like a frozen wave, above her. She could see the basket sitting by the handar and ran across the stones and sand to pick it up.

It wasn't until she was close to the handar that she realized that the basket was empty. It was still yesterday's basket. Today's had not yet been brought. She stood, biting her lip, and looked around. The valley was deserted, save for the ever-present eagles above. To go back to Sandwriter and return later seemed a foolish waste.

She decided to wait in the cave, safely out of sight, as Sandwriter would have wished, and hope that the people in the village would remember the offering before the sun set. Probably they too were upset by what had happened that day. Perhaps it was one of the villagers and not a passing traveler who had been hurt when the kroklyn bolted. That would account for the delay.

She crouched in the shadowy cave and waited patiently. Waiting was something she had become very accustomed to over the last years. How long is it since I was last in this cave? she wondered. How long since Sandwriter stripped me naked and cut off my hair? It had been a terrible but meaningless gesture then, when she was ten years old. Now she knew what Sandwriter had done. She had stripped her of everything that was hers, so that she could remake her in the Sandwriter image. So that one day she would be ready to take up the power when the present Sandwriter became part of the Great Dance in death.

"Why, I have nothing at all," she said aloud, and the cave echoed her voice. "I *am* nothing at all. I have lost count of the seasons and the years. I don't even know how old I am or what I look like."

She felt her face with her fingers. It was lean, the cheekbones sticking out like shelves beneath her eyes. Her hair had grown again, but raggedly and, without Nan's loving brushing, it was rough to the touch. She looked down at her body. It was no longer a child's but that of a thin, almost gaunt, woman. Her hipbones jutted out, and she could count her ribs. How ugly I must be, she thought. If ordinary people could see me, they would laugh at my ugliness.

Outside a pebble moved and Rania tensed. On

hands and knees she crept to the opening of the cave. A man was kneeling by the handar, a man with golden hair and beard, dressed in a tan robe. How long he stayed there! What was he doing? She waited, her heart pounding, until at last he stood up, the empty basket in his hand. He was young and tall and very good-looking, she saw in the single glimpse before he turned his back and strode across the valley to the slope of the Great Dune.

She waited in the shadows until he was out of sight and then darted out to take the full basket and leave the empty one. With the torch in her other hand she wended her way through the mountain to the northern cave where Sandwriter still lay sleeping.

It was almost sunset, so she left the food basket and squatted on the mat by the cave door to meditate as Sandwriter would have done. Only then did she take the food from the basket. Her mouth watered. *Three* loaves of bread! And what figs! Full enough of juice to burst. She ate as much as she could hold and then lay in the darkness on her mattress, gazing out at the star-filled night.

Every time she shut her eyes, pictures flashed into her head. Sandwriter, standing, her arms outstretched, with blue light dancing from her fingertips. Sandwriter, entranced before the fire, remote in some other world. Sandwriter pointing out a healing plant, the pattern of stars in the winter sky, the shape of windblown sand.

A faint gray light had crept into the cave when Sandwriter stirred and sighed. Quickly Rania rose and fetched a mug of water. The old woman drank greedily and laid a hand on Rania's arm, as if in thanks, before her eyes closed again.

That is the very first time I can remember her touching me with love, thought Rania. She shivered in the dawn chill and crept back under her blanket. How strange that the touch of her hand on my arm should make me want to cry. I don't understand. But there was a feeling, like a heavy stone, somewhere inside her chest.

At dawn she rose and sat by the cave opening to greet the morning sun. Its color was strange today, a bloody red that was not natural. As it moved up toward the zenith she noticed that the sky had a brassy, brittle look. The air was very still and silent except for the shrill trilling of a desert beetle that seemed to grow louder and louder as the morning wore on.

Rania busied herself by chopping vegetables and making a soup. As soon as Sandwriter woke, she would need nourishment. When that was done she sat beside the old woman, occasionally taking her hand, limp and fragile as a small bird. Inside her chest the stone weight seemed to grow heavier.

There was food left from yesterday, a whole loaf of bread and a lot of fruit, so Rania ate again, until it was gone. She had never eaten in the afternoon before.

Or had she? Surely when she was a little girl there were meals more than twice a day? She had a vague memory of sauces and sweetmeats, but perhaps they were only in her imagination.

Sandwriter was still sleeping quietly, so she took the empty basket and a fresh torch and once again went through the mountain passages to the south. This time the basket was already there at the foot of the handar. She left the torch inside the cave and went out to pick up the fresh offering. The heat smote at her and the air was still and breathless. She looked uneasily at the sky. Something was wrong. It was almost as if Rokam itself were sick. As Sandwriter was. But that was fanciful, wasn't it?

As she exchanged her empty basket for the full one and turned back to the shelter of the cave, something fell at her feet. She picked it up and hurried on. Only in the shadows of the cave did she pause to look at what she was holding. A billet of firewood? No, it had human features, carved roughly in the hard thornwood, and a brown homespun robe, the mirror of the one she wore herself. It might have been cut from the same cloth.

She dropped her basket and cradled the doll in her arms. In the unconscious movement her memory suddenly filled with a procession of all the other dolls she had held and loved. One by one they passed before her eyes and she found herself saying, "You. I choose you." And it was the freckled cloth doll that she had taken from the palace on her last day in Malan, because it reminded her of Stefril. *Stefril!* How many times had Rokam turned since she had last seen him? And Nan. And Mother and Father. Slowly her legs gave way under her and she sank to the sand, the stiff wooden doll clutched awkwardly in her arms. The tears poured from her eyes and sobs tore from her dry throat in ugly bursts of noise.

"Princesses don't cry." She heard Nan's voice in her ears but she couldn't stop. She cried until her head throbbed and her throat was sore. But the weight had gone from her chest and she could think clearly. She looked around. The shadows in the valley were long. If Sandwriter were awake she would wonder what had happened to her.

She scrambled to her feet, still clutching the doll. "I can't let you go," she said aloud. "You're mine. I'm going to call you Stefril and she shan't stop me having you."

She looked around the empty cave and quickly dug a hole in the dry sand close to the inside wall. She laid the doll within the hole and smoothed the sand over the top. It's like a grave, she thought and shivered. But it's the only way.

Sandwriter was awake when Rania returned. She drank the vegetable soup that Rania had prepared, washed her face and hands and squatted on the mat by the door as if nothing unusual had happened. For once Rania was thankful for her silence. When she should have been meditating on the setting sun she thought instead about the doll and about Stefril. How much he must have grown. She probably wouldn't even recognize him. Or he her.

She switched her mind from that painful thought to Freedom. Freedom was Stefril's pony now, but she could, in her imagination, pretend that he was still hers. That he had somehow crossed the sea and the desert, that he was waiting for her outside. He would whinny in the night and she would creep out of the cave, out of Sandwriter's power, climb on his back and ride far away. Only where could she go? If Freedom took her home, Mother and Father would send her back. Not all her imagining could change that one unalterable fact: that Mother and Father had given her to Sandwriter.

She blinked her eyes and stared at the last rays of the setting sun. I won't cry, she told herself firmly. Sandwriter has never seen me cry. She lay on her hard mattress for a long time that night, as rigid as her new wooden doll, before she was able to fall asleep.

Next morning the threatened storm had arrived. The sky was a hideous orange color, the sun only a faint smear of light. The wind blew unceasingly and sand hissed against the mountainside.

Perhaps Roshan is angry because I took the doll, thought Rania. I should confess to Sandwriter what

I've done. But she closed her lips firmly. No, it's the only thing that's really mine in the world, and she'll never let me keep it.

As the day wore on and the hissing of the sand and the screaming wind never ceased, she felt as if her skin were all nerve endings with the sand scratching at them.

"Oh, why can't you stop the wind?" she suddenly snapped. "You have the power. You brought the storm . . ." Her voice faded as the old woman turned to look keenly at her. She could feel her cheeks burn with guilt and she had to turn away.

"It will pass," Sandwriter said mildly, and Rania hoped that she had seen nothing wrong. I must get away, she thought.

"Let me go for the offering basket," she suggested. "I went yesterday and the day before, while you . . . slept."

"No one will be able to leave the village today. There will be no basket."

"But—"

"Why are you angry, child? A day's fast will do us no harm. As for the storm, do you not yet understand that every action each one of us takes affects not only those close by but, in a small way, as small as the weight of a single feather or grain of sand, the whole of Rokam? Two days ago I called upon the rain gods to save Atmon, because he is the headman of the village and his son Atbin is not yet wise enough to take his place. Power is a terrible gift. I forced the rain to come out of season. Today's sandstorm balances the wrong I did."

"Wrong? But you saved a man's life."

"At a price. Now come and sit beside me and meditate, child. The time will pass more quickly and you will not notice the lack of food."

Is it true? Rania wondered, as she obediently sat beside Sandwriter. Does every action affect the whole of Rokam? Even hiding a doll? Yes, it's true. Hiding my thoughts and feelings from her is making me feel different inside. How far will it go? My doll is just a little secret. It can't be all that important.

The time passed with maddening slowness and she caught herself fidgeting, playing with her fingers, twisting a lock of hair. Sandwriter looked at her, eyebrows raised, and she blushed.

"My legs ache so," she lied. "May I walk through the tunnels? That will be almost as good as walking outdoors."

Sandwriter's eyes seemed to strip the pretense away, but all she said was, "Why don't you go to the pool, child? It will calm your restless spirit."

Rania didn't answer. She knew that she wouldn't go to the pool. She lit a torch and sped through the passages to the cave by the valley.

The wind was like a river in spate, pouring down between the mountain and the Great Dune, carrying sand and dust high on its waves. She placed the torch carefully out of the wind, so that it filled the cave with cheerful light. Then she uncovered the doll and brushed the sand off it.

"Don't be afraid, my precious Stefril," she murmured. "The storm will soon pass. Meanwhile we'll have a picnic in here, that's what we'll do. What shall we have? How about gazelle meat in wine, and vegetables braised in butter. And afterward— I know! We'll have chepa tartlets and zaramint candies."

The thought of food made Rania's mouth water. Next time I come, she thought, I'll save some of my bread. For the time being imagination had to take the place of a real feast. She peopled the cave with her family and friends. She sang her favorite songs and told the doll her favorite stories. The more she talked and sang, the more she remembered of her past life. Sometimes she wondered where the doll had come from.

"Are you from the person who brings the offering, the man with the beard? He's very good-looking. Could it be he? Or perhaps it was Atbin's mother. She sounded very kind."

Something rustled in the darkness beyond the torchlight and she stiffened. But it was only a sand-mouse, escaping from the storm. It sat on its hind legs, its fan-shaped ears pricked forward, its nose twitching. "Oh, do stay," she whispered. "Don't run off."

She wished again for food—you can't feed a real

sand-mouse on imaginary pastries, however delicious. "Next time," she promised, "I'll bring something for you. Oh, I hope you'll be here."

She blinked. The mouse had almost vanished in
the shadows. Rania was suddenly aware that it had
grown very dark. She looked up in alarm to see that
the torch had almost burnt out. Hastily she laid the
doll in its hiding place and covered it over. She
snatched the torch and walked as quickly as she
dared along the tortuous passages through the
mountain.

She had passed the second fork when the flame
flickered and went out. At best the world underground was small, limited to the circle of light cast by
the flame. Now it shrank to no more than the space of
a timid footstep forward. To an outstretched hand
feeling for the openings.

If I only had something to burn, she thought. But
she had nothing at all except for her coarse robe. She
pulled threads from the worn hem and laid them
across the glowing tip of the torch. They flamed
briefly and curled into white worms of ash. Now it
seemed even darker.

All about her the mountain groaned and creaked.
There were other, unfamiliar, sounds. She stopped
and listened, realized that they were the sound of her
panting breath, the thud of her heartbeat. She forced
herself to breathe slowly, to control her rising panic.

"I have been through these tunnels a hundred

times. If I think hard, I shall know exactly which way to go."

In her mind she built a careful map and placed herself within it. When it was clear she began to walk slowly forward, the cooling torch thrust out in front of her. It should be twenty paces or so until the next obstacle, a set of three rough steps leading downward.

She walked forward as boldly as she dared: eighteen paces, twenty. Twenty-one. The problem was that her mental map was built upon the memory of a lighted tunnel, her strides through it long and confident. Distance has quite a different meaning in the dark, she realized.

Step by step she shuffled forward. Her foot slipped and she lunged, trying to recover her balance, and fell, skinning her knees as she flopped forward, her torch rolling away into the darkness.

For some reason this panicked her more than the fall itself, and she spent useless time feeling for it in the blackness. At last she got to her feet and felt about her with her hands. Shape and space had vanished and she felt dizzy until she touched the cold roughness of stone and was able to set off again, her left hand against the wall, her right hand extended to the emptiness ahead.

"The next turn on the left is the passage that leads down to the pool." She tried to keep the tremor out of her voice. "Once I've passed that opening I'll be halfway. After the left-hand passage I come to the dangerous fork. I must be careful to take the passage on the right."

Encouraging herself forward with a whispered monologue, Rania passed the passage to the pool, passed the false turn that led to a deep pit, crept on hands and knees, sweat rolling down her face, over the stone bridge where the walls of the passage had crumbled away into some chasm far below until, at last, she came to the final flight of steps.

She climbed them with wobbling legs. Now she could see the texture of rock ahead, and her hand, palely lit, pressed against the wall. Now there was the comforting glimmer of the fire. She could see across the cave the coppery light beyond. She could not believe that it was still daylight. She felt as if she had been in the darkness for days.

She leaned against the wall, out of sight, and steadied herself. She wiped a damp hand over her face and rubbed the palms of her hands on her robe.

"Are you there, child?"

"Yes, Sandwriter." She was able to keep her voice steady as she walked into the cave. She knelt beside the old woman on the mat by the entrance and sat back on her heels, her hands folded neatly in her lap.

I won't tell her, she promised herself. And next time I'll be more careful.

6

*S*ometime during the night the wind dropped. By morning the sky was clear, although the sunrise was bloody red. Once the morning meditation and lessons were over Rania asked permission to meditate by the pool.

Sandwriter looked at her for a long time, and Rania felt her cheeks become hot. Her hand felt surreptitiously for the bread that she had saved from breakfast and hidden in her robe. At last Sandwriter nodded.

"I—I'll take the empty basket and bring back today's offering. It'll save you a journey. You are still tired."

Sandwriter said nothing and Rania snatched the

empty basket and a torch and fled from the steady gaze of those piercing eyes. Her guilt seemed to follow her like the darkness of the underground passages through the mountain. She found herself stopping, turning, the torch high. But there was nothing to see.

When she reached the cave she uncovered the thornwood doll and brushed the sand from its face and clothes. "There, Stefril. Now I must take the basket outside. Oh, I am so hungry. We didn't have a basket yesterday because of the storm, so we've been on half rations. Now let us see if we can trick the sand-mouse into coming back." She broke the precious ration of bread into small crumbs and laid them in a line from the pebbles outside the cave to the corner where she played with the doll.

She sat quietly, Stefril in her arms, and before long her patience was rewarded. The mouse appeared, its great ears turning to and fro, its nose twitching. It ate the crumbs, one by one, until the last crumb. It was now so close that she could see the silkiness of its whiskers, and the trembling of its body as its heart beat.

Suddenly it was gone, leaving the last crumb. Rania picked it up and ate it as slowly as she could. Oh, how hungry she was! Perhaps the man would come soon with the offering. She could take it to Sandwriter and persuade her to let them have a meal, just a little meal, before sunset.

She got to her feet and walked to the cave entrance. He was there! She shrank back into the shadows. He was standing facing directly toward her. He hadn't seen her, had he? She peered cautiously out of the shadows. His skin was a goldish brown and now, with the sun gleaming on the sweat on his shoulders and chest, he looked like one of the bronze statues in the palace garden. His hair and beard were sun-bleached, a shade lighter than his skin.

Something attracted his attention, something high above the mountain, and he leaned back to look. His eyes flashed blue, the blue of her father's. Of the old chief. Of Atbin. Then his hand went up to his forehead, shading his eyes, and she wondered if she had imagined it. *Could* it be Atbin? Could that shy youth have changed into this glorious man? How many years *had* she been hidden away in this mountain, growing thinner and dryer and lonelier?

Suddenly the doll cradled in her arms became no more than a billet of wood. It wasn't dead. It had never really been alive. She put it away in its hiding place and mechanically smoothed the sand over it. Then she took the torch and the full basket and walked through the mountain passages to Sand-writer.

She still saved bread secretly and she still slipped away to the valley cave whenever she could. After a few days of feeding, the sand-mouse was almost tame. It would sit beside her, washing its whiskers, while she talked to it. After a time Stefril began to be alive again too.

She built a pretend palace of lines of pebbles and one day found a small stone, smooth and caramel-colored like Freedom. She built a stable next to the pretend palace for him to live in.

"Climb up in front of me, Stefril. We'll ride to-gether." In her imaginary world Stefril was still four years old. Then the pebble would become a mighty steed, galloping across the desert, back toward the real palace in Malan. She could almost feel its muscles move under her, feel the wind cooling her hot fore-head.

Often, without her meaning to, the imaginary Stefril would become Atbin and it was he who was rescuing her. She would feel her cheeks grow hot and she would try to push the thought of his golden shoulders and his blond beard out of her mind. They tended to return though, at inconvenient times, when she was supposed to be meditating or gazing into a dish of water or the fire. She never saw pictures in the water or the fire anymore. She never saw anything except Atbin. It became increasingly diffi-cult to hide her secret from Sandwriter.

One day the magic fell apart and the secret was discovered. She had fed the sand-mouse, who would now sit on its tiny haunches for the last piece of bread and remain to finish it, turning it over and over in its hands, nibbling delicately. It always trembled, though, as if fear were just around the corner. Perhaps that's why I love it so, thought Rania. Because I understand.

The mouse had run off and she was playing with Stefril and Freedom. She had imagined them at the edge of the Small Sea. She could see the dock and a sea gull swooping over the water. It screamed—

A small shrill sound. Outside the cave. She was just in time to see the great desert eagle rise from the ground, flapping furiously to gain height, the limp form of the sand-mouse in its talons.

It's my fault. I lured it here and tamed it. I killed it.

What had Sandwriter said? *Every action, however small, has its effect on the whole of Rokam.*

She threw the caramel stone across the cave. She kicked the walls of the palace and the stable apart. Then she slumped against the cave wall and cried all the tears of all the dry years she had spent with Sandwriter. She cried until there were no tears left. The torch flared up, flickered and went out. When Sandwriter came searching for her at sunset she was asleep on the sand, her head pillowed on one arm, the other wrapped around the wooden doll.

The old woman held her torch high. Her wise eyes noticed the scattered pebbles, the tear stains, the doll. She bent and picked Rania up, with surprising ease for a woman who seemed so frail, and carried her back through the tunnels and laid her on her mattress.

Rania never stirred. Sandwriter broke twigs of incense-wood into small pieces and lit a fire close to the door of the cave. She blew it into flame. She sat close to it, inhaling the sweet smoke. She stared into its embers until, by sunrise, she knew what she must do.

Rania woke from muddled dreams to find the sun flooding the cave with light. It was already afternoon. Why had Sandwriter let her oversleep? That had never been allowed, even in the early days, when she had to be shaken awake.

Beside her mattress was a loaf of flatbread and a cluster of dates. She drank three glasses of water and ate the dates and part of the bread. The last portion she was just about to hide in her robe when she remembered. The sand-mouse was gone. And the magic of imagination with it. She crouched by her bed, head down, and fought the tears.

The faint sound of bare feet on sand made her turn. She scrambled to her feet. "Sandwriter! I—I'm sorry. I overslept."

"It is not important, child. Come, sit with me on the mat. I have something to say to you."

Rania sat obediently beside the old woman. Her heart was pounding and her hands felt cold. She *knows*, she thought. What will she do to me? Will she be very angry?

"I was a grown woman when the previous Sandwriter called me to join her," the old woman said slowly. "It was a difficult thing, to leave everything behind, my family, the hope of husband and children. All the normal little things, the ordinary things. But it was not a choice. I *had* to go. For Rokam.

"She taught me everything she knew and, ten years later, she returned to the sand of Roshan and I became Sandwriter. I held Rokam in my hands for more than thirty years, waiting for a sign. It came sixteen years ago, when your mother Antia and your father Jodril wrote their names in the sand of the Great Dune. I knew then that their child would be the next Sandwriter. All I had to do was to wait.

"When you were ten years old I dared wait no longer. I was seventy-six. I was afraid that I might die before I had a chance to teach you everything I knew. So I sent for you and tried to teach you as the old Sandwriter taught me, to let go, to forget myself, to become strong in the service of Rokam. I did not understand how difficult it might be for a child. Forgive me."

Rania tried desperately to think of something to say. If only the old woman would hold out her arms to her. If only it were possible for her to make some small human gesture, then it would be all right. But she sat as if she were carved out of sandstone, like the handar in the valley.

"I went to the village while you slept and talked to Shudi. She is a sensible woman and knows more about children than I possibly could. Her cousin, Methra, is the widow of a sailor and lives in Monar. She keeps an inn. You are to go and stay with her."

"Leave *you*?" Was it a punishment or a reprieve? "For—for how long?"

"Until you choose to come back. Until you desire the teaching I must give you."

"But suppose that's never? Oh, please, let me go home instead. I'll never be what you want. You don't know. I've cheated and lied. I've closed my mind against your teaching, against Roshan . . ." Her voice choked with tears.

"Hush, child." The hand that touched her shoulder was as light as the touch of a sand-mouse, but it dissolved the stone that had lain so heavily on Rania's heart. "You have been with me for four years, child. If, in a year, when you are fifteen, you can convince me that I was wrong in choosing you, you shall go home. But"—she went on quickly as Rania turned a shining face toward her—"I do not believe I was wrong."

The next caravan rested at the oasis of Ahman a ten-day later and, when it set off the following morning, Rania went with it. She was wearing a new desert robe and carried a small bundle with a dress suitable for Monar, both made for her by Shudi.

At sunrise Sandwriter had accompanied her through the mountain to the valley and up to the crest of the Great Dune. "There is your escort." Sandwriter pointed to where a lone figure, swathed in desert white, waited beside a kneeling kroklyn. She put her hands on Rania's shoulders. "Go now, child. Always remember to do what seems right. Never forget that every action, however small, touches all of Rokam, as a drop of water, falling into the sacred pool, spreads across to the farthest edge."

She turned, without waiting for any farewell from Rania. Her dusty brown robe seemed to melt into the sand of the dune. In an instant she was gone. Rania descended the farther slope, her bundle under one arm, feeling strangely lonely and rejected. But I *wanted* to leave. And this *is* an adventure, she argued with herself.

The waiting figure turned. The teeth flashed white in the tanned face.

"Atbin?"

"You remember me? I didn't think you would, Princess."

"You've changed," she said shyly. "But I guessed it was you. Only you mustn't call me 'princess' anymore. I'm only Sandwriter's apprentice. No, not even that. I am just Rania."

"Very well, 'Just Rania,'" he teased. "Let me help you up. Are you still afraid of kroklyns?"

She was actually able to laugh a little. "No, not anymore. I was only a child then."

"And now?" He helped her into the saddle and climbed up behind her.

"I am fourteen. I am a woman."

"Yes, Princess . . . yes, Rania."

He flicked the kroklyn, lurching, to its feet and they set off to meet the rest of the caravan as it rounded the eastern flank of the red mountain. The sun had just risen and their shadows ran westward along the sand like pointing fingers. Rania's eyes followed. Once they had reached the north side of the mountain she tried to turn in the saddle. Could she see, among the many holes and cracks on the slope of the mountain, the particular one that marked the entrance to their cave? And was Sandwriter sitting on the mat, watching her leave?

She waved, a small stirring of her hand, nothing more.

"You did that once before," Atbin suddenly said.

"Did what?"

"Waved your hand like that. Like a small bird trying to escape. I never forgot it."

"I don't remember. But you . . . Atbin, did you carve that doll for me?"

"It was nothing. I made it years ago, after— I see now that you were too old for—"

"Oh, no. It was wonderful. It was the first thing of my own . . . the only thing. Thank you, Atbin, thank you very much indeed. Oh!"

"What is it?"

"I just remembered. I left it in a cave one night, a ten-day ago."

"I could find it and have it sent on the next caravan."

"No, no." She laughed. "Sandwriter wouldn't want me to—"

"What is it like, living with—with her?" Atbin whispered.

Rania couldn't answer. She didn't know how to. She shook her head wordlessly.

"I'm sorry," Atbin said stiffly. "Mother warned me to watch my tongue. 'She's the apprentice of Sandwriter,' she told me. 'Not a little girl.' I know these are sacred things. I didn't mean—"

"Tell me about Monar." Rania hastened to change the subject.

"It's a great place, almost as large as Lohat, with a fine harbor. It's always busy, because the fleet that fishes the great sea is harbored there. And there are ships from the Far Isles as well as from Kamalant. And fine kroklyns. My father always buys the kroklyns for the village from the herds at Monar."

"You've been there with him?" Rania smiled at his excited voice. His muscles and beard were a man's, but the boyish enthusiasm was just as she remembered.

"Oh, I've never been to Monar. But I've heard about it all my life."

"Perhaps we can both explore it before you have to return."

"Yes, indeed," he said politely, and Rania wondered if he would rather be on his own, drinking in inns, and ogling the pretty girls. She looked down at her thin hands protruding from the folds of her desert robe. I'm certainly no one to boast of, she thought ruefully.

That night she slept on the hard ground with the drivers and other passengers: a man and wife traveling from Lohat to visit their grandchildren. They ate only mishli, a pasty gray travel food, with fresh dates and figs from Ahman; but to Rania it was like a wonderful holiday with the kindest, most handsome man in the world for company.

"Do you remember our last journey?" she asked Atbin. "I had a tent with cushions, and gazelle meat and chilled fruit to eat."

"This is very different."

"I am less afraid this time." She smiled at him. "Do you suppose— When will I see you again?"

"Mother says I am to return in a year to take you back to Sandwriter."

"A year? A whole *year?*" Rania couldn't keep the disappointment out of her voice.

It was his turn to smile. "You would like to see me sooner?"

Rania blushed and nodded, suddenly shy.

Atbin seemed to be concentrating on tracing a

pattern in the sand with his fingers as he asked casually, "Rania, do you *want* to be Sandwriter?"

"No, I don't. I dread the thought."

"Such power, though. To be mistress of Roshan."

"I don't want that kind of power. I don't want to have to make the kind of choices Sandwriter must make . . ." Her voice rose and the merchant couple from Lohat looked across at her in surprise. She lowered her voice. "It is not only that, Atbin. It is the loneliness. No one to talk to, no one to share the burden with. I think it has changed her. She isn't any longer quite . . . human. I don't think she remembers anymore how to love. And . . ."

"Go on."

"I don't want to spend my whole life alone," Rania stopped, then said in sudden self-awareness, "I want a husband. And children."

"You would rather marry than be Sandwriter?"

"Of course! I'm just an ordinary human girl. I'm not strong and distant like—like *her.*"

"Of course, if you *don't* become the next Sandwriter, you'll go back to the palace, won't you?"

Rania began to draw idly on the sand. "I don't think I want to go back to that life anymore," she said slowly. "I think I would rather live like an ordinary woman in Roshan."

He laughed. "You don't really know how ordinary people live. You have always been extraordinary all your life, as a princess, as Sandwriter's apprentice."

Her chin went up. "I was with ordinary people on the caravan from Lohat. Do you remember what the kroklyn driver said?"

He shook his head, his eyes laughing at her. "It was four years ago. Forgive me!"

"*I'll* never forget. He said I was a true daughter of the desert. And there's this trip to Monar. Sleeping on the ground, eating travel rations. That's ordinary, isn't it? Well, isn't it?"

"I think you're extraordinary wherever you are," he said softly and she felt her cheeks getting hot.

Later that evening, as they rolled themselves in their blankets beside the fire, he said, "I wonder if Sandwriter has sent you to Monar for that reason."

"What?" she answered sleepily.

"To learn what an ordinary life is like."

No, Rania thought to herself, as the smell of burning thornwood drifted past on the night breeze, Sandwriter is angry because of what I did. How strange. That makes me feel so sad and yet at the same time I'm happier than I've been since I was a little girl. I wonder why. Just before she fell asleep she thought: of course, it's because of Atbin.

The merchant and his wife complained bitterly of the hard sand under their well-covered backs and of the quality of the travel food, but to Rania it was as she had told herself, an adventure. The floor of the cave had been as hard, and her rations with Sandwriter had been much more meager than the food they shared now.

Above all, her days were full of delightful companionship. Atbin talked to her of ordinary human things; she learned a great deal about the cultivation of beans and the care of cisterns and wells, as well as the names and personalities of all Atbin's uncles, aunts, and cousins. But five days in the saddle she was not used to and, when Atbin lifted her down from the saddle on the evening of the fifth day, she was weary and saddle-sore, her teeth gritty, and her eyes smarting from the ever-present wind and sand.

The house where the caravan had stopped was built of mud bricks, but it was unusual in that it was two stories high, with a flat roof above and an outside staircase and gallery. It was painted a brilliant blue with orange trim, and it sagged a little toward the neighboring house, as if the two were sharing a disreputable secret.

The cobbled street led steeply down toward the harbor, bright with gaudy-sailed fat-bellied ships bobbing on the turning tide. There were people everywhere, riding lemas whose hooves struck sparks off the cobbles, pushing handcarts with noisy rattling wheels, walking three or four abreast, arms carelessly slung over each other's shoulders. Above the noise of hooves and cartwheels was the continuous clamor of voices.

As Rania shrank back from the noise and gaudiness, a woman rolled out of the door of the inn. She was enormous and, like her house, both bulged and sagged. She was dressed in a striped tent of pink and purple and yellow, her hair pinned up hastily on top of her head.

"Welcome to the Fair Wind, one and all. Enter, sir and madam. Why, who do we have here? Shudi's young friend, Rania, I'll be bound!"

Her voice was as thick as winter honey. She held out her arms in welcome and Rania fell into them unquestioningly and buried her face in the soft bosom. "Nan, oh Nan!" she found herself crying.

"Bless you, I'm no one's nana. I'm Methra, widow of Longstaff, late captain of *The Fair Wind*. Me inn's called after his ship. There, there." A plump hand patted her shoulder vigorously.

Rania drew back, her cheeks hot. "Forgive me. I forgot . . . you are very like someone I once knew."

"It won't be too long before we know each other as well, I'll be bound. Now come aboard, my girl, you and your baggage. What? Just one small bundle? Well, Shudi sent word your ways might be different, but is this indeed all you own? And who is this handsome young man with the great beard? If I were only five years younger! Ah, me! What, you're little Atbin? I would never have believed it. Come aboard, both of you."

Still talking, Methra pushed Atbin and the dazed

Rania into the inn. The huge room was cool and dim, with walls a handspan thick and windows of bubbly green glass. It smelled of tarred rope and dried fish, of spices and beer. An overpowering smell but exciting rather than unpleasant. It smelled alive, Rania decided, whereas Sandwriter's cave smelled only of sand, cool rock, and the occasional faint windborne scent of zaramint.

"This is the dining room and beyond is the tavern. You'd best stay clear of it, Rania, my girl, when the sailors are in port; though now I look at you, I suppose you'd be safe enough—such a scrap, all skin and bones and dark eyes, like a bird that's fallen from its nest. Come through to the left, the both of you, into the kitchen."

Here were smells of onion and garlic that hung in ropes from the ceiling, shiny red spice-pods in baskets on the walls, a fresh fish glistening silver on the scrubbed table. An overpowering smell of fish from a pot on the stove. Three dusky shadows detached themselves from the gloom and wreathed around Methra's legs, lean brown and black cats.

"Greedies, greedies!" Methra laughed as she lifted the pot off the stove. "Lovely fish heads for supper. Wait, wait, too hot for little mouths yet."

The cats followed her to the table and stretched their lean bodies upward. Their eyes gleamed at the silvery fish. Methra tapped their noses lightly until they dropped to the ground again.

"Through here is my bedroom. There's a spare one beyond. Atbin, you can sleep there until the next caravan leaves. As for you, Rania, my girl, you can have the little attic upstairs. It's away from the tavern noise and has its own little stair, see." She opened what had seemed to be a cupboard door, to disclose a narrow flight of stairs.

"Go on up and get out of those dusty clothes. You'll feel the better for a wash and change before supper."

Staggering with tiredness, Rania climbed the steep stair on stiff legs. It finished in a square opening in the ceiling. She mounted and found herself in a room crowded with boxes and old furniture. It was lit by a very small window in the east wall and a somewhat larger one to the south, overlooking the roof of the next house.

In the angle between these two windows a space had been swept clean and covered with a grass mat. There was a simple wooden bed, a chair and a small chest upon which was placed a basin and jug. There was a slop pail and, under the bed, a matching chamber pot. The bedcover had been knitted in the same creamy color as the mat. The whole effect was fresh and welcoming.

Thankfully she stripped off her dirty desert robe, poured cool water into the basin and washed herself from head to foot. Then she undid the bundle that Sandwriter had given her. In it was a blouse and skirt of simple homespun. As she shook them out something fell to the floor and skidded out of sight.

Before she could look for it, the voice of Methra boomed up the stair. "Supper's on the table, Rania. Come eat it before it gets cold."

She tied the fastening of the skirt and ran quickly downstairs. Beside Atbin, already sitting at ease, were two girls of about fifteen or sixteen who were introduced as Tekla and Hattia. Hattia was a large pale girl with a slow smile. Tekla, on the contrary, was sharp-faced and quick. She greeted Rania with a wink.

"So you're to be the latest slave. Watch out! Methra's terrible for getting the last crumb of work out of a body."

"Tssk, you're ahead of me, girl." Methra frowned. "I've not spoken to Rania, so hush up, do."

Rania could make no sense out of this exchange, so she smiled politely and concentrated on the food. The meal began with bean soup, laced with spices that left Rania's mouth aflame. This was followed by the baked fish, its skin charred and split to show tender pink flesh, its inside stuffed with chopped vegetables.

Methra heaped Rania's plate. "You're as thin as a ship's mast, my girl. Eat up."

Rania tried to finish, but years of abstinence had shrunk her stomach. "I'm sorry. I can't eat another scrap."

"Are you sure? Off to bed with you then. I can see your eyes are shutting already. Here's a candle. Mind you pinch it out before going to sleep."

"Thank you. Goodnight. Goodnight, Atbin. I—I will see you before you go, won't I?"

"Of course. I said we'd explore Monar together, didn't I?"

"Oh, well as to that—" She smiled vaguely and, taking the candle, went upstairs.

She put the candlestick down carefully on the chest and looked out of the south window. The sun had long since set and beyond the rooftops was the desert, a blackness unrelieved by lamplight or candle. Beyond the desert, where the horizon met the sky, a million stars blazed.

"Are you awake, Sandwriter?" she whispered into the darkness. "Are you thinking of me at all? But why should you be? All I have ever been was the promise of the next in line."

She sighed. How true that was. Never by word or gesture had the old woman ever shown that Rania meant more to her than the one upon whom she could lay her burden. That had been the worst part of the last four years, she realized. That *that* was all she was.

She turned from the windows and undid the tape that held her skirt. It slipped to the floor. As she stepped out of the ring of cloth and bent to pick it up, she remembered that something had fallen from her bundle. Something heavy enough to skid away into the shadows.

What could it be? She took the candlestick and set it on the floor so she could look around. Here was a bundle of rags. There a roll of dust. A sheaf of old sailing charts. What was that? She groped in the space between two boxes and drew out the doll that Atbin had made for her.

She got to her feet and put the candlestick safely back on the chest. Such a funny doll, so crudely carved, its dress no more than a patch of cloth with a hole cut for the head, a piece of twine about its middle. But Atbin had made it for *her*. She ran her fingers lovingly over the features. Then she blew out the light and scrambled into bed.

The sheets felt cool and smooth. The mattress was stuffed with wool. She lay on her left side, her eyes toward the south window, the doll cradled in her arms. Downstairs Methra would be sleeping. And Atbin. Soon he would have to go home. *He* had a home to go to. She did not.

How noisy the street outside was. People sang and laughed. A group went by, shouting at the tops of their voices. The bed rocked under her with the rhythm of the kroklyn's gait, but she couldn't sleep. It was stuffy in here and her back ached from the soft mattress. She rolled over and stared at the ceiling. "Oh, Sandwriter, why did you send me here?" she whispered. "Is it a punishment for what I did?"

The wooden doll dug into her ribs. Who had put it into her bundle? It could be nobody but Sandwriter. Why had she done that? Surely it must mean that she had been given back the doll as a sign—permission to have, to hold, to love. Only wisely.

"She does love me. She does."

Rania buried her face in the lumpy mattress and wept.

7

"Fresh fish! Flounders and flippers! Who'll buy my fresh flounders and flippers!"

Rania groaned and sat up, hot and unrefreshed, feeling that she had hardly closed an eye all night. Where was that awful din coming from? She scrambled out of bed, put on her blouse and skirt, and looked out of the small window overlooking the street. It was packed from side to side with people, shoving, waving their arms and shouting.

Has something terrible happened? A war or an earthquake? She leaned perilously far out of the window and saw a woman dig an elbow as large as kroklyn's knee into the ribs of a man dressed in a red jerkin and yellow and blue striped socks. She saw a woman selling cheeses the size of cartwheels and another with a basket of purple seaweed on her head. A man struggled through the crowd with wreaths of wooden clothespins around his neck; another was laden with bales of greasy wool.

Rania backed away, her hands over her ears. How can they endure such a racket? she wondered. Then curiosity drove her back. What bright colors they wore and how cheerful they all seemed. The pushing and shoving, the elbowing and jostling, all seemed to them the natural way to behave.

"Rania, are you awake, my girl?"

As if anyone could sleep through this racket! she thought. "Yes, Methra." She ran downstairs to the kitchen.

"Eat up your breakfast." A plate covered with a large grilled fish was slapped on to the table in front of her. "The girls have started work already, but here's Atbin begging me to let you have the day off so you can explore Monar."

"Oh!" She looked up, her face bright. "Really, Atbin?"

"Really, Rania." He mocked her gently. "There's a caravan leaving before dawn tomorrow. I must go back with it. But we have today and Mother gave me a length of cloth to sell. She says I may keep half of what I can get. So hurry. The day's half over."

Rania gobbled her fish and drank a glass of water. "There, I'm ready."

"You're never going out looking like that, are you? Come here, my girl." Methra made her stand still while she forced a comb through her tangled hair. "I don't know. You'd think you'd never *looked* in a mirror by the state of this. I can't do much with it now, but here's a bit of red ribbon to tie it back."

"Thank you. You're *very* kind."

"Don't worry about your hair. Come on." Atbin caught her arm and, with the bolt of cloth under his other arm, hurried her out into the bustle of Monar. They struggled through the crowd, asked the way to Cloth Lane and set out. After a few false starts they turned into a street lined with stalls, many of them laden with exotic fabrics finely woven of wool from the sheep on the Far Isles where, Atbin told her, it never stopped raining.

He ignored these and went to a stall selling good plain stuff. When he showed the owner his cloth she ran it expertly through her fingers. "This is from the loom of Shudi in the village of Ahman. Right, aren't I? I never mistake cloth. She's a good weaver, Shudi, and I'll offer you ten coppers for the length."

"*Ten!* For Shudi's work! You won't find a flaw in it if you searched all day. Her work's worth double that."

"Double!" the woman screamed, and Rania drew back in dismay, but Atbin grinned.

"Double it is. Twenty coppers." He held out his hand.

"I never said that. You cheeky lad. Tell you what. I'll give you twelve."

"Eighteen!"

"Robbery. Fourteen." Atbin shook his head and stood, the cloth in his hands. "All right." She sighed heavily. "I'll split the difference. Fifteen. My last word, you rascal."

"Done," said Atbin. He tucked eight of the coins safely into his belt and shook the remaining seven in his hand. "And these are ours. Let's see what we can spend them on, Rania."

They found, by the scent of hot bread, sugar syrup, and roasting tega nuts, the street where sweetmeats were sold. Fascinated, Rania watched a red-haired woman roll and twist pieces of dough and drop them into a pot of sizzling fat. She lifted them out with a wooden strainer and dropped them in sugar syrup.

"Oh, Atbin!"

"How much for a bagful?"

"Two coppers, young man."

"Two! Have a heart. I've only seven coppers to spend on my girl all day."

She laughed. "One copper then, but it'll be a small bag."

Atbin smiled his shining smile and Rania could swear the bag was as large as any of the others she sold. They walked slowly down the cobbled street toward the harbor, eating the hot, fluffy sweetcakes, and licking their sticky fingers.

The harbor was the most exciting place Rania had ever seen. There was a ship from the Far Isles in port, the small dark sailors chattering to each other in fast, high voices as they carried ashore baskets of fine cloth, jewel stones from their shores, and carved ivory from the tusks of the great sea beasts that swam in the oceans east of Roshan.

A fishing boat docked, its hold full of blue and yellow fish, squirming and sliding, as sailors clad only in knee breeches, their shoulders streaked with sweat and fish scales, loaded them into baskets.

There was a ship from Kamalant, its funnel and paddle wheels setting it apart from the sailing ships of the rest of the world. Rania had to admit that it wasn't nearly as beautiful, in fact it was almost ugly. The Kamalant sailors seemed to keep themselves apart from the bustle and joyfulness of the rest.

"Think they're too good for the rest of us," Atbin commented.

"Because they use steam instead of sail?"

"I suppose so. But if they had as little wood to burn as we do they'd have stuck with sail too."

"Could I ask one of them about—about Mother and Father, about Stefril?" she asked Atbin.

"You *could*, but I don't think you'll—" Atbin stopped. Rania had already darted off and was talking to one of the sailors. He followed quickly and had his arm protectively around Rania just as the man laughed and reached out to pinch her.

"Sorry. No offense," the man muttered. "But what does she want asking me about them in the palace? Why, yes, had dinner with them last ten-day, as a matter of fact."

"I just wanted to know—"

"As far as I know they're all alive and kicking. Now off with you. I've got work to do."

Rania bit her lip.

"It's all right, Rania. It's only sailor talk. Come on. There must be lots to see and I'm getting hungry again."

They bought hot meat pies and freshly squeezed juice and then walked up and down the cobbled streets, gazing at embroidered dresses and jewelry, some fit for a queen, some cheap stones hanging on chains. Atbin bought one of these for Rania with the last of his coppers: a red stone, streaked with gold powder. He hung it around her neck.

"There. Now you won't be able to forget me."

"As if I could. Thank you, Atbin." Her hand went to the stone. It felt warm against her skin.

The bay was streaked with red and the cobblestones were golden when they walked slowly, hand in hand, up the main street to the inn.

"I'll never forget today, Rania."

"Neither will I."

"The caravan leaves early. I won't see you again—"

"Until next year, you said."

"Unless I can find a reason for coming back. Things

are different since I looked after the village when Father broke his leg. He knows I'm a man. He may let me bring more of Mother's weaving and some baskets to sell next time we need a kroklyn."

"You got a good bargain this time, didn't you?"

"I think so."

"The women like haggling with you, because you're young and good-looking."

Atbin blushed and laughed. "I'd better not tell my father that, or he won't let me out of Ahman until I'm married."

"He wants you to marry a village girl."

"Maybe. Not necessarily." He took her hand. "Rania, if you do decide to lead an 'ordinary' life, would the village of Ahman be too ordinary for you?"

She could feel her hand trembling and tried to draw it back. He held it more tightly. "No, don't," she whispered. "You're teasing me, aren't you? I'm . . . nothing. I'm as skinny as a bird. My clothes . . . my hair. Oh, I noticed how people looked at you and how they *stared* at me."

"That's just what Sandwriter made of you. I remember you as you were four years ago. I know how you could be again."

She shook her head. "I can't say anything one way or the other. I don't know. I haven't tried this 'ordinary' life. You were right. I was being silly. Perhaps I'm not fit to work the way most women work."

"Then we'll wait until I see you again. Will you agree to that?"

She nodded and he softly kissed the tips of her fingers and held open the door for her.

"I'll write," she said.

He laughed. "No one in the village can read. But you can always send a message by a kroklyn driver."

Then he vanished into his room and she lit a candle from the lamp on the kitchen table and went slowly up to bed.

She woke with a start in the morning. It was daylight. The caravan with Atbin in it must have left long before. She looked out of the south window. The smooth expanse of the desert was interrupted by a small line of black dots, halfway to the horizon. She lifted a hand in farewell, while her other hand went to the stone, warm at her throat.

Once downstairs there was no time to mourn his leaving.

"There's a lot of work to running the Fair Wind and we must all take a hand in it," Methra told her. "Don't think that I'm not happy to give a home to any friend of Shudi's, but she'd be the first to understand that food doesn't just jump onto the table nor the sheets wash themselves. Anyway Tekla's scrubbing the tavern floor this minute and Hattia is collecting the sheets to wash. We've our own well, thanks be, with good sweet water. So what are you sitting there for? The sooner we get started, the better."

"Yes, Methra." Rania tried to finish the huge helping of fish on her platter, but in the end fed the scraps to the cats, who had appeared from nowhere and were weaving passionately about her ankles.

". . . and those cats get plenty to eat with fish-head stew once a day," Methra went on, without turning around. "If you go a-spoiling them they'll be too fat and lazy to catch rats. Oh, yes, even the cats earn their keep around here, don't you, pussies?"

"Sorry, Methra. I've finished, so what can I do?"

"Tidy your room and empty your slops in the street drain. Then help Tekla in the tavern."

Rania cleared her scraps into the bucket by the sink and ran upstairs to smooth the cover over her lumpy bed. Negotiating the narrow stairs with a slop pail in one hand and a chamber pot in the other was difficult, but crossing the crowded street to the drain was worse.

She returned, blushing, to the inn, to find Methra watching her, arms akimbo, shaking with laughter. "Next day pick a quieter time, like before sunrise," she advised.

In the tavern she found Tekla scrubbing the floor. "Oh, there you are at last. Take this pail and fill it with hot water from the stove. Here's soap and a brush. You can start on the tables."

Rania fetched water, dabbed the brush into the cake of soap, and began to push it across one of the sticky tables.

"Not like that! You'd think you'd never held a scrubbing brush in your life. Dip the soap in the water and rub it across the table. Now get the brush good and wet and scrub with both hands." She pushed the brush vigorously to and fro until the brown beer stains vanished and the white wood gleamed. "Then take a wet cloth and wipe it off. Rinse and wipe as you go, all right? Come on, we've not got all day, as *she* would say."

"Don't we rest at all?" Rania panted, drying her wrinkled hands on her apron after the last table was scrubbed and pushed back into place.

"What do you think?" Tekla's eyes twinkled. "We have to empty the pails, right? Come on and you'll see. Make sure *she's* out of the way." She darted through the inn door, lugging a heavy pail of dirty water, Rania after her.

Once the pails were emptied into the drain that ran down the center of the street to the harbor, Tekla slid through the crowd and around the corner. Soon they were in the sweetmeats' lane again.

"Oh, I ate those yesterday. They were wonderful."

"Have some now."

"I've no money."

"She's got to pay you sometime, hasn't she? You can pay me back later." Tekla bought a bag and they walked slowly back eating the hot sweet dough.

"For goodness' sake lick the syrup off your mouth or Methra'll have something to say."

She did anyway. She was waiting for them at the door, large and terrifying. "Just where do you think you've been?"

"Emptying the slops." Tekla showed the pails. "The tavern's shining bright. Looks lovely—"

"I've been waiting for you, right in front of this door."

"Did you ever see such a crowd? We could hardly get through to the drain." Tekla slipped nimbly past Methra into the inn, Rania close behind her.

"Off with you to help Hattia with the laundry, you lazy wretches," Methra shouted after them.

"How dare she call us lazy. I never worked so hard in my life," Rania whispered.

Tekla laughed. "She's not so bad. She never beats her servants like some do. And she pays a just wage if you keep up to the mark. But you call this morning's chores work? You're a strange one. Honestly now, did you ever do a day's work in your life before?"

"Well . . ."

"You worked hard enough, but as if you'd never held a scrubbing brush in your life and taking twice as long as natural."

"I'll get better," Rania promised, as Tekla took her hand and pulled her through a door at the back of the kitchen, into a paved yard enclosed by the wall of the house on one side and a high mud-brick wall on the other three.

At a low stone trough close to the well Hattia was kneeling, scrubbing sheets with a cake of soap, slapping them against the stone side of the trough, rinsing, and scrubbing again.

"Here at last," she said over her shoulder. "Slipped off to the fried-cake stand again, I suppose? You'll do it once too often, Tekla, and Methra will throw you out. Then what'll you do?"

"I'll manage. Don't scold, dear Hattia. I saved a cake especially for you."

Rania stared. She was sure they had finished the whole bagful. Tekla winked at her.

Hattia gave a virtuous sigh. "You know I won't waste my mistress's time on eating or idle gossip. Nor should you. You two can wring out and hang the sheets I've finished."

Twisting the wet sheets between them, shaking out the creases and hanging them on the lines which crisscrossed the yard, was pleasant work compared with scrubbing out the tavern. When the laundry was done they had a lunch of bread and cheese and beer, after which they were set to remaking the twenty beds upstairs and then to chopping vegetables for supper.

It wasn't until she climbed stiffly upstairs to bed that night that Rania had a moment to think about Atbin. She knelt by the southern window, her arms on the sill, and looked out over the dark desert. They were both out there somewhere, Atbin sleeping by the thornwood fire under the stars, Sandwriter in the cave. One of them must be her future, but which? I'm too tired even to think, she told herself, and tumbled into bed.

Each day was more or less like the first. Cleaning out the inn, scrubbing the sheets, and preparing the meals. A ten-day after Rania had come to stay at the Fair Wind, Tekla and Hattia received their wages, but there was nothing for her. She gathered together her courage and asked Methra for some money.

"Money? But you're not a servant like Tekla and Hattia, my girl. Aren't you my guest, a friend of my dear cousin Shudi? Let's not spoil our friendship with sordid talk of *money*."

"I work as hard and as long as Tekla and Hattia. And I eat at the same table."

"But you have your own room, my girl, for which I don't charge you a single copper. Separate, too. Why, it's almost an apartment."

"A corner in your attic?" Rania stared at Methra as boldly as she dared, her heart pounding.

At length Methra laughed. "I've been feeding you too well, that's certain. The milky miss who rode into town with Atbin a ten-day ago wouldn't have answered me back. Well, I don't want to see you unhappy. I'll give you eight coppers every ten-day. I know it's not as much as the others get, but you're not as quick and you *do* get bed as well as board. That's my last word, so no argumentation."

"Thank you, Methra." Her hand closed over the coins. How grand, she thought. The first money I ever earned—eight whole coppers.

"That won't go far," said Tekla bluntly. "You already owe me two for fried cakes."

"Here they are. That leaves six. I must have a dress, Tekla. No one in Monar wears a blouse and skirt as plain as mine."

"You certainly *do* stand out. Leave it to me. I'll find you something pretty for no more than six coppers. Then you can save up for a pair of shoes and a shawl. It'll start getting cool in the evenings soon."

Between the laundry and kitchen chores they ran down to Cloth Lane, where Tekla went from stall to stall, ruthlessly pulling out pieces of cloth and discarding them, until she found what she said would be perfect for Rania: a piece of cloth striped in blue and red, a dark red that matched exactly the pendant Atbin had given her. Then she found a white blouse with a flaw in the warp running down the front, so she was able to beat the seller's price down to Rania's last two coins.

"They're lovely. I'm so grateful. . . . But who do I get to make the length up into a skirt? And how much will I have to pay?"

Tekla stared at her accusingly. "You mean you can't sew either? No more than you could cook or scrub or wash the clothes? Whatever were you brought up for? You're no more use than a princess!"

Rania's cheeks flamed. "I'll learn, if you'll only teach me."

Tekla giggled. "To tell the truth. I'm a terrible seamstress myself. My mother's despair. But don't worry. We'll ask Hattia. She sews perfectly—of course!"

With a lot of ripped-out stitches and pricked fingers, Rania learned to sew a straight seam, so that the next time the girls had an afternoon off she proudly wore her blue and red skirt and the white blouse, down the front of which the clever Hattia had embroidered a stripe of red to hide the flaw. She had washed her hair and rinsed it in rosemary tea, tying it back with the red ribbon Methra had given her, and she felt the equal of any girl in Monar.

I just wish that Atbin could see me now, she thought, but the ten-days slipped rapidly by and there was no message from him. Caravans came and went. Rania saved enough for a shawl, for now winter was approaching and, although Monar was closer to the equator than the oasis, the nights were often chilly. She also bought a pair of shoes, the first she had worn since leaving Kamalant four and a half years before. Her feet felt strange and constricted in them, but she looked very smart.

Winter already, she thought, and tried to count on her fingers the number of ten-days since Sandwriter had sent her away. How strange her hands looked, brown and strong, with calloused palms, broken nails, and ragged cuticles. Hard-working hands. Like Atbin's mother's, she guessed.

What do I look like? she asked herself. Has the rest of me changed? There was no looking glass in the attic, but she pushed her hair back from her face and leaned over the laundry trough to see her reflection. Her cheekbones no longer stood out under hollow eyes. She was pink and almost plump, and her eyes sparkled with good health. Sandwriter would never recognize me, she thought. I hardly know myself.

As she stared the water turned cloudy as if with the laundry soap. Then it became as clear as a mirror in which she saw the red mountain, the steep entrance to the cave, a figure standing in the entrance. It was as clear as if she were looking through a doorway into that other world five days' ride across the desert.

Sandwriter, she thought. Holding the weight of Rokam in her hands while I am wasting time with sheets and floors, thinking about clothes and sweet-cakes instead of being beside her, learning the great secrets. Her heart thudded like a drum and the whole world seemed to stop turning for an instant.

"What *are* you dreaming about, Rania? I've asked you twice to pass the soap."

She jumped and blinked. "Sorry, Hattia, I didn't hear you." She glanced at the others and back to the water. Had they noticed anything? There was nothing now but the rough stone trough and soapsuds floating on the water.

"She's mooning over her true love from the oasis, so don't criticize her; you're just as bad."

"Hush, Tekla." Hattia scrubbed the sheets so hard that her pale cheeks got quite pink.

"I didn't know Hattia had a true love," Rania said later, when she and Tekla were hanging up the sheets.

"He's a fisherman's son. They're saving for a boat of their own. Once they have it, they'll be married."

"How long will that take?"

"Forever, I should think," Tekla answered carelessly. "Hattia's been saving to get married ever since we started work here. Pass me that last sheet, will you?"

8

*R*ania knelt at her southern window, her arms folded on the sill, watching the last rays of the sun paint the desert crimson. What had happened to her? Had that been a true vision? And why had it come, out of nowhere, unexpectedly and unprepared for?

The light began to fade from the sky. Without conscious thought Rania found herself repeating the familiar words of the farewell to the sun ". . . and protect Rokam as it turns in the Great Dance, protect its people that all may lead their lives for the good of others."

Surely Sandwriter would be ashamed of her life since she had come to Monar. "I eat too much. I sleep too long. I spend my days chattering and my earnings on clothes and cakes. I never spend time in meditation."

Four years, she thought. Four years of training and learning, and it slips away so easily. Her hand strayed to the red stone hanging around her neck. But if she *were* to marry Atbin, this year in Monar had been a hundred times more useful than her four years with Sandwriter. Before coming here she did not know how to cook or clean or sew, the needful things of ordinary life.

Atbin or Sandwriter. Sandwriter or Atbin. The pendulum of a great clock, ticking out the alternatives. She went to sleep unresolved, but she woke before dawn and slipped quietly out of bed to watch, as she and Sandwriter had watched, the coming of the new day to Roshan.

She felt something beginning to unfold within herself, something strange and beautiful, although not without danger. What is it? she asked herself. Are the powers I learned from Sandwriter coming to the surface, like water seeping up through the rock, stronger than ever? And how am I to use them?

She decided, in the small time of day that was hers, to practice again what Sandwriter had taught her. Before dawn and in the dusk before dark, she knelt on the attic floor gazing into the water of her washbowl. At first there was nothing but her own face, lit in the flickering light of her candle, but she persevered and began to see movement, glimpses of life in Monar, such as she might see looking out of her window or walking down one of the cobbled streets.

She saw a woman brushing her hair beneath a fig tree, a child skipping outside a door carved with curly fishes, a ship setting sail. Then a particular face appeared. It was a young man's, with the red cheeks and steadfast blue eyes of a sailor, distinguished from the tens of Monar sailors only by a small triangular scar on his right cheek. The face began to haunt her.

"What's the matter with you, Rania? You're as slow as a slug today."

"Sorry, Tekla. Just thinking."

"Then stop thinking and hurry up with that floor so I can push the tables back. I want to buy cakes and take them down to the harbor. The fishing fleet is in."

Rania scrubbed the floor so fiercely that the old boards shone. "There, that's done. Are you going home to change? I'll have a quick wash and meet you outside."

Down at the harbor they munched their sweet-cakes and watched the fishermen unloading their catch and haggling with the housewives who had come down to meet the boats.

Tekla suddenly waved and pointed. "Look. There's Lothril."

None the wiser, Rania followed her along the wharf, threading her way among heaped nets and crates and barrels. In the last boat a young man, naked to the waist, was stooping over his catch, sorting it into baskets.

He straightened up when he saw them and smiled at Tekla. "So where's Hattia?"

"Obviously she didn't know your boat was in or she'd be here. She left work ahead of us today. Look, here she comes now."

The plump Hattia ran along the wharf. "I'm late!" she panted. "You're back early. And I'm quite out of breath. I ran all the way from the cloth store."

"The wind was favorable and our holds were full. How are you, Hattia?"

"Very well. Is your father in good health?"

Tekla nudged Rania. "Let's go. The conversation isn't going to get any more exciting."

Hattia giggled. "Tekla, you are terrible."

As they turned to leave, Lothril swung a basket of blue flounders onto the wharf. As he straightened Rania saw, with a shock of recognition, that he had a small triangular scar high up on his right cheekbone.

That night Rania's hands trembled as she poured water into her basin and sat patiently waiting for the water to grow still and to show her the meaning of her vision of Lothril. She sat until her back was stiff and her body chilled, but the water showed her nothing.

Perhaps that too is a sign, she told herself, and

continued to rise before dawn to greet the sun and to meditate, as Sandwriter would be doing in her cave, five days' journey to the south.

Meanwhile winter came, bringing the cool currents north and with them the shoals of big fish. Now all the fishing boats in the fleet were readying themselves for the voyage around the northeastern bulge of Roshan to catch the great craybot. Even on the small smacks, such as that owned by Lothril's father, the men were busy day and night, caulking seams, splicing ropes, mending torn sails. There was big money in the craybot catch. Just one big fish would pay for the year's upkeep of a man and his family.

"Buy a new dress," Tekla persuaded Rania. "You can't wear that one blouse and skirt for ever."

She picked out a simple design in red wool with stripes of fine black woven through the fabric. "There. With your pale skin and dark hair you look like a princess. All the boys will be after you—"

"Don't, Tekla!" Rania would have put the dress back, but Tekla caught her wrist, put down the money and dragged her away from the stall.

"You're hopeless. I don't know why I put up with you."

"I didn't mean— It was kind of you to help me choose it, and it *is* beautiful. But—"

"Don't you *want* to look pretty? With all the sailors out there, now's the time!"

"No!"

"There's someone else, isn't there? That good-looking man who brought you from Ahman? Ah-hah. I know your secret."

"Then keep it, Tekla." Rania managed to smile, but inside she was in turmoil. How was she supposed to read her life? She had meditated faithfully and had seen nothing in the water. The power seemed to have vanished as inexplicably as it had returned. Did that mean that Sandwriter was rejecting her? That she should choose Atbin after all? When she first wore the new red dress, saw how the bodice fitted over her breasts and snugged in at her waist, she couldn't help wishing that Atbin were there to see her in it. The pendant he had given her matched the dress perfectly.

She pushed the image of herself and Atbin out of her head and continued to meditate and gaze into the water. A ten-day later she had her reward. The visions returned. Now she saw the fleet, sails rounded by the wind, pennants fluttering cheerfully. Then the picture changed to the open sea, angry gray waves running high, their tops torn off in wind-blown spume.

The following night all she saw was a single ship, a small smack tossing in the waves, its mast snapped like a thorn twig. The picture came again and again and she prayed for a sign, something to tell her what she should do.

At last the message came. The same small boat, the

same storm, but now the body of a young man lying on the bottom boards, close to the fallen mast. She could see the rain running off his upturned face and the small triangular scar high on his cheekbone, just below his closed eyes. It was Lothril!

She paced the floor of the attic all night and, as soon as it was light enough to see, she slipped out of the inn, her shawl around her shoulders, and ran down to the harbor.

The big ships must have left in the night and the harbor was almost empty. She ran from wharf to wharf, her bare feet slipping on planks slippery with fish scales, looking for Lothril's boat. Surely she wasn't too late? No, there it was, over there.

"Lothril, I must talk to you."

"Something is wrong? Hattia?" He jumped ashore and caught her by the elbows.

"No, no. Hattia's fine. Lothril, you mustn't go out this time."

He stared and then laughed. "It's a joke, isn't it? Tekla's, I'll be bound."

"It's not a joke, I swear. It's deadly serious, believe me. Lothril, I have the gift of dreaming true. I've been dreaming of the fishing fleet and your boat especially. Last night I saw it dismasted and you lying dead. It's a warning, Lothril. Please heed it, for Hattia's sake."

He pushed her away. "And what shall I tell my father? That he should sail without me? He couldn't haul in a craybot single-handed. Or should we both skulk in the harbor while the rest grow rich?"

"I can only warn you of what I saw. Please don't leave. It would break Hattia's heart if anything were to happen to you."

"If I don't catch a craybot we won't be able to get married for another year." He jumped back into the boat and looked up at her with a smile. "But you can wish me luck if you've a mind to, Rania."

She ran back to the inn, getting to the door out of breath just as Telka and Hattia arrived for work. "Where *have* you been?"

Rania explained. ". . . you've got to persuade him to stay home, Hattia. He won't listen to me."

"I should think not. I've never heard such non-sense in my life. Dreaming true indeed!"

"It's not exactly dreaming. It's . . . something I was trained to do, seeing pictures in water. A gift, you could call it. . . ." Her voice died away. "You don't believe me, do you? You won't do anything about it."

"Lothril would think I was crazy. One more good catch, that's all we need. Then Lothril will be able to afford his own boat and we can get married. Be-sides—" She looked up. "Just look at that sky. Not a cloud in sight."

"It could change fast. There's a haze to the south."

"I suppose you can tell the weather too, know-it-all?"

"As a matter of fact I *can*," Rania snapped and ran into the inn, bumping into Methra inside.

"Where have you been, my girl? Well, never mind the explanations now. You've missed your breakfast. Better start on the tavern floor. Where are those other two? Late again, I suppose. . . ."

The three girls worked in chilly silence all day and, at its end, Telka and Hattia went off together, leaving Rania alone.

She threw her shawl over her working dress and walked slowly down to the harbor. The tide had risen and was falling again. The wharves were deserted except for the boat of two toothless mariners who made their living netting sprats in the bay for bait. Overhead seabirds screamed hungrily. The seaweed growing on the wooden pilings under the wharves moved slowly up and down on the tide—like the hair of a drowned man, Rania thought, and turned away shivering.

"I've wasted my time meditating. I saw true but no one would listen. Now Telka and Hattia won't even speak to me. Who else have I? Mother and Father abandoned me. Sandwriter sent me away. Atbin— Oh, how I wish Atbin were here. He would under- stand and help me."

A wave of self-pity engulfed her. Then a thought, mean and bitter as a snakebite. *Lothril will die and then Hattia'll be sorry she didn't listen to me.*

Her hands went to her mouth. "I didn't mean it. O rain gods, hold back your anger from the fishing fleet. Save Lothril. I will do whatever you want."

The tide sighed and heaved against the pilings. The sea gulls screamed. As she turned and walked slowly home a dark line of cloud banded the southern sky and crept slowly northward.

In the middle of the night the wind tore through the attic room, knocking the thornwood doll off the chest of drawers with a clatter. Rania, who had fallen into an exhausted sleep, woke with a start. She scrambled out of bed and struggled to close the wooden shutters across the windows.

By morning the storm was savage. Hattia did not come to work and Telka arrived, coughing, eyes streaming from the dust that was everywhere. As soon as the tavern was clean, Methra sent her home again.

"Every ship is at sea, may the gods help them. Nobody in their senses will leave home on a day like this. I'll close the inn until the storm is over." She sighed heavily and Rania wondered if she was remembering her dead sailor husband. But perhaps she was just thinking of how much money she would lose while the inn remained closed.

Rania spent the rest of the day huddled on her bed listening, between uneasy dozes, to the wind screaming through a gap in the shutter.

It was not until sunset the following day that the wind dropped. Rania walked down the strangely silent streets to the harbor, her shawl tight across her chest. It was crowded with women, some standing

alone, most in family groups. Hattia was with Lothril's mother and the younger children.

The sea heaved uneasily up and down, sloshing
over the wharves one minute and sinking the next to
expose the weeds and barnacles that covered the
lower part of the pilings. The slosh and suck of water
had a kind of rhythm. *I told you so. I told you so.* And
then: *You should have listened. You should have listened.*
She tried to push the sounds out of her head. They
were of no comfort to anyone.

When it grew dark the harbormaster tied torches to
posts along the wharves. Their flames rose and fell in
the gusts of wind. Lothril's mother took the children
home, but Hattia remained. Rania walked along the
wharf to join her, her shadow leaping forward and
back as she passed from the light of one torch to the
next.

"How did you know?" Hattia turned on her. "How
could you know?"

"It's a skill I was taught. I don't know."

"A terrible skill."

"Yes, Hattia, it is."

"We were planning to get married this year, if he
and his father caught a craybot."

"Perhaps I was wrong, Hattia. He may be safe."

"Out of a clear sky . . . the storm came out of a
clear sky! But you knew, didn't you? If he doesn't
come back I'll—I'll never speak to you again."

"But—" Rania swallowed and bowed her head. "If

· 151 ·

it helps you," she managed to say. She walked back up the deserted street to the inn.

Methra had already locked up and she had to knock at the door and wait to be admitted.

"What's the matter, me dear? You look as if you've been crying."

"The wind in my eyes," Rania lied and went upstairs.

She didn't sleep for a long time, although she couldn't blame the wind for keeping her awake, and she was wakened by Methra's voice calling to her shortly before dawn.

"What is it?" She splashed her face with water, scrambled into her blouse and skirt, snatched up her apron, and ran downstairs.

Methra was in high excitement. "Quick, eat a bite now. There'll be no time later. A ship has been sighted, praise be. If the wind is kind they should all be safe in harbor by nightfall. And we'll be run off our feet. I can't count on Hattia. She'll be down at the harbor, waiting, I'll be bound. Oh, there'll be such celebrating tonight! I'm going to make my special fish pies and . . . yes, my fish roll-ups. Hurry up and sweep the tavern and dining room and dust the furniture. Thoroughly, mind. That dratted sand'll be everywhere. Then make sure all the rooms are ready with clean sheets and towels and fresh water in every jug. There'll be other ships than our own coming in after a storm like that, and my inn'll be as full as it can hold."

Rania grabbed a piece of bread and stood with the broom in her hand. Perhaps Lothril is safe, she thought. Perhaps I didn't see true.

"I just hope Tekla gets here soon. I need every hand I can get. Now, for goodness' sake, Rania, stop dreaming and get to work."

Later, as Rania helped Tekla make up the beds, a new thought struck her. If Lothril *does* come safely home, my visions have no meaning. I cannot be Sandwriter's successor. I will be free to marry Atbin.

"What are you dreaming about, Rania? You know, when you smile like that you look really beautiful. Pass me the corner of that sheet."

As they were polishing the beer tankards early in the afternoon, a woman's voice came from the street. "The fleet's in! They're home, praise be!"

"Methra, please may we go? Everything's clean and ready."

"Have you put out all the cutlery in the dining room?"

"Yes, Methra."

"And enough clean platters?"

"Every last one you own, Methra."

"Then off with you. Oh, it's a thankful day! I wish I could come too, but I've my pies to watch."

Tekla and Rania tore down the deserted street. The

wharves were already thronged with almost every soul in Monar. They stood in silence, watching the ships limp home, commenting only in whispers at the sight of a snapped boom, a sail torn in two.

Eager hands seized the mooring ropes and fastened them around the bollards. Eager hands reached out to help the men stumble ashore, their clothes stiff with salt, their eyes reddened with wind and spume, their faces stony with fatigue. Now the voices rose, the stories were carried through the crowd.

". . . came on us out of the blue. Never seen a storm like it . . ."

". . . and we'd just hooked our third craybot and hauled it in . . ."

"Third! What luck!"

"Luck indeed. It was the weight in our hold stopped us from rolling over. But we lost a sail . . ."

". . . and old Starff broke his arm trying to free the fallen boom . . ."

Slowly the chatter died away as, one by one, families walked up the hill, arms about each other. Now the fish processors were scrambling aboard, hauling the huge fish onto the wharves. By nightfall the whole catch would be cut up and the slices hanging in the smokehouse.

Now barely ten women remained, their faces sharp, their eyes staring out to sea. Hattia was among them, and Lothril's mother.

Rania clutched Tekla's arm. "Have none of the small boats got back yet?"

Tekla shook her head. "They're slower. They carry less sail. Perhaps by nightfall . . . We'd better go back. Methra will be needing us."

She was right. By dusk every man had bathed and changed and was celebrating with his wife or girl. Barrel after barrel of beer was emptied while every last pie and fish roll-up was eaten and Methra had to turn her hand to frying fresh craybot steaks.

Out in the kitchen Rania and Tekla washed dishes and pots in a never-ending cycle. When the hot water from the stove was used up they had to scrub the dishes in cold.

Tekla groaned as she hung up the last wet dishcloth. "I'm dead. I think I'll sleep for a hundred years!"

"A hundred years, is it? An extra hour in bed I'll allow you for your work tonight. But I want you here scrubbing floors and tables after that. Oh, what a crowd! Oh, what a profit we've made today!"

Rania's knees were shaking and her back ached, but sleep was far from her mind. As soon as Methra was out of the way, she slipped out of the inn and down to the harbor. It was again lit with torches, but tonight they burned clearly without a flicker. The sea, too, was calmer and only a slight swell remained of the savagery of the storm.

"What news?" she asked an old woman huddled against a mooring post.

"Two boats put in a while ago." Rania followed her pointing finger. A mess of torn sail and tangled shrouds. Neither boat belonged to Lothril's father.

"How many are still missing?"

The old woman counted on her fingers, naming off family names. "Five still to come. Yes, five."

Rania waited. Slowly, during the long night, the small boats came limping in. One. Two. Three. Four.

By the time the midnight constellation had dipped toward the west the harbor was deserted, save for Hattia and Rania. It was chilly, and she crouched down against a mooring post and pulled her shawl tightly around her shoulders. The stars began to fade. She dozed fitfully.

A scream wakened her and she was on her feet in an instant, dazed and shivering. Had it been a seabird? She blinked and saw Hattia standing at the end of the wharf. Out in the bay a gray shadow crept closer. Now it was close enough to see that the mast was gone. Now she could see that the boom had been lashed to the stump to make a temporary rig, from which a small triangle of sail hung.

She ran along the wharf to join Hattia. The boat came alongside. It was exactly as she had seen. The jagged scar of the broken mast. Lothril lying in the bottom of the boat with his eyes closed, his face the gray of the sea.

With a wail Hattia jumped down into the boat. She knelt beside Lothril and cradled his head in her lap.

"Easy does it, girl," Lothril's father croaked. "He ain't dead yet. Just knocked silly by the falling mast, as far as I can tell. But he's breathing. And we got two craybot!"

Rania leaned back against a post, suddenly dizzy. "Thank you, rain gods, for answering my prayer," she whispered. She straightened up and took a deep breath of the fresh dawn air. Then she walked slowly up the hill and knocked at the inn door.

"What are you about, waking me up at this hour after a day like yesterday's?" Methra grumbled.

"I'm sorry. I had to wait till the small boats got back. They're all safe now, every last one. Even Lothril is safe."

"Lothril? What's *Lothril* to you, my girl?"

Rania laughed weakly. "Nothing. And everything."

"Oh, go to bed, for goodness' sake. You make no sense at all."

He's safe, she thought, as she stood by the south window, looking across the desert. Does that mean that my water-seeing is meaningless?

"If my visions have any meaning, then I *am* supposed to be the next Sandwriter," she said aloud. "But I was wrong, because Lothril is safe. So perhaps I'm free to marry Atbin after all. I just don't know. And I'm too tired to work it out."

9

*W*hen Hattia came to work, she greeted Rania with unexpected warmth and a box of expensive sweetmeats. ". . . and Lothril's mother Basti will be honored if you will come to a small celebration as soon as Lothril is fit."

"How *is* Lothril today?"

"I think he will recover soon, but his head aches and he says that he is bothered by seeing two of everything."

Tekla giggled at the thought, but Rania frowned. "That could be more serious than it sounds. He should lie still, Hattia, until the symptoms leave. And there is a remedy, the juice of the red-flowered cactus, mixed with water, that will lessen the pain."

She stopped suddenly. "I—I'm sorry," she stammered. "I didn't mean to interfere. It may not be suitable. It is only something I learned when—when I was living in the desert."

Hattia grasped her hands. "Oh, please. I am most grateful. I will run home and tell Basti. The red-flowered cactus, you say? How should it be diluted?"

"One part of juice to four of water," Rania said mechanically. "And drunk no more than six times between one sunrise and the next."

Hattia nodded and ran off. Tekla whistled in a vulgar way. "Well, I don't believe it! What a change of heart! She'll be eating out of your hand next."

Before Rania could think of anything to say, Methra sailed into the room, talking at top speed as usual. "What are you girls *doing*? Do I see pails of hot water? Do I see brushes and soap? No, alas, all I see is a filthy floor and two gossiping girls. Two! No Hattia this morning? All the more work for the two of you. To work, to work. Quick! Quick!"

There was certainly little time for idle gossip or speculation on the circumstances of Lothril's safe return, for which Rania was thankful. The Fair Wind was packed to the roofline with sailors whose homes were not in Monar but who had put into safe harbor to repair their ships after the storm. Rania worked with a concentrated fury intended to keep her own thoughts at bay.

She was just stripping off her dirty apron at suppertime when a thundering came at the inn door. "I'll go."

"Room for a tired traveler?" came the voice from the shadowy street.

"There's not a spare bed in the—" Rania stopped, peered out, and then pulled the young man into the dining room with a gasp. "Atbin! When did you arrive? And what are you doing here? Oh, I am so happy to see you."

"Rania? Is it really you? How . . . how beautiful you have become! I hardly recognized you . . . in . . . the dark, I mean."

She laughed and held up a lamp. "Here I am then. Am I as beautiful in the light?"

"More so. And you said— You *did* say you were glad to see me?"

Rania blushed and put the lamp down. "You haven't answered *my* questions yet."

"Yes, let me see. When did I arrive? One moment ago. The caravan is on its way down the hill this instant. What am I doing in Monar? Why, I'm trading my mother's weaving for another kroklyn."

"Your father trusted you with *that* mission? Oh, Atbin, that is wonderful."

"Yes, he was pleased with what I earned on the small piece of Mother's work I brought last time. Now he's entrusting me with all the trading. He will be the headman all his life, Rania, but later it will be *my* job, you know. It's a small village, and compared with

Monar not very exciting. But it's a good life, and the wife of the headman is to be respected."

"Atbin, why are you telling me this? What are you trying to say? That you want *me* to be— You haven't changed your mind?"

"Changed my mind? Rania, I've thought of nothing else. Have you decided whether you will return to *her* or make a life for yourself? For us?"

Rania gave a short laugh and pushed her hair out of her eyes. "My choice was riding upon an event. No: I would return to Sandwriter. Yes: I would marry you—if you still wanted me. But—"

He grasped her hands. "The answer is 'yes'?"

"The answer is 'maybe.' Perhaps I am intended to make up my own mind and not rely on signs. I don't know." She sighed.

"'Maybe' will do for now. That and a bed for the next few nights. But you said the inn was full?"

"Not for you, of course. Come into the kitchen. We were just having supper. Methra, just look who's arrived!"

Next morning Atbin managed to persuade Methra to let Rania have some time off. What sweet talk he used she didn't know, but Methra beamed and almost pushed her upstairs to change into her good dress. "Hattia and Tekla will manage the work. But only for the morning, mind. I will need you this afternoon to help prepare dinner."

"Does she always drive you girls like that?" Atbin asked as they walked, hand in hand, down the cobbled street.

"She sounds fierce, but she is a good woman at heart, though too fond of money. Where are we going?"

"First to Cloth Lane to get the best price I can on Mother's weaving. Then you shall help me choose a good kroklyn with the profits."

The kroklyn stables were situated just within the walls of the town, close to the eastern gate, where the screams and smells of the animals would be least disturbing to the residents. With a considerable sum of money heavy within the sash of his robe, Atbin introduced himself to the son of the owner, a young man called Rathbin, and they began to haggle.

It is an interesting process, thought Rania, seating herself comfortably on a bale of sweet straw to watch. They walked up and down the line of animals, looking at their feet, their teeth, the line of their necks. Now and then Atbin would stop to look more closely at one or another animal, but Rania felt that this was just a show and he was really interested in the one he seemed to disregard. It's like a complicated dance, she thought, with pride at Atbin's shrewdness.

If he had been brought up in a palace, she thought, he would have become an important statesman. Since he has been brought up in a desert village, he will be the headman and an astute trader and organizer too. She glowed with pride when the two men shook hands, the money was handed over and the kroklyn was theirs.

"I will tattoo its ear with your mark today and you can take it tomorrow."

"Tomorrow? Must you leave so soon?" She burst out.

"I can stay three days. There won't be another caravan leaving until then. I will pay you a stabling fee for the extra two days, of course." He turned to Rathbin.

The young man spread his hands. "Consider it in the price of the beast, Atbin. I hope you will come to my stable again."

"Do you have any money left?" she asked in a whisper as they walked back to the center of town.

He tested the weight of coins in his sash and grinned at her. "What may I buy my girl? Jewels? An embroidered shawl? Just tell me and it's yours. Today is a special day."

"A bag of fried cakes," she laughed. "And then I must go back to work."

They walked back to the inn munching the sweetcakes and licking the honey from their fingers. Hattia was waiting with an invitation from her mother.

"For both of you to come to the celebration tonight."

"Then Lothril is better?"

"Your medicine was like magic." Hattia's voice faltered on the last word and she looked at Rania with something uncomfortably like awe.

"It's nothing. A remedy an old wise woman taught me, that's all. I'm glad he is better. We'll be happy to come, won't we, Atbin."

Atbin, who had been hoping for an evening alone with Rania, smiled politely and said he would go back to the market and choose a housegift for Lothril's mother.

"And we must get on with the laundry. There's a mound of it to finish before we start the vegetables."

"Is Lothril's home close by?" Rania asked as they scrubbed and rinsed the sheets. "Will we find it easily?"

"Anyone will tell you. You understand it's my home now. I live with Basti and Tofril."

"With your future husband's parents?"

"Of course. Isn't that the custom where you come from? As soon as a couple are promised the girl goes to live with her future mother and helps her in the house. This gives the mother a chance to see if she is well-trained. I share the small children's room and help Basti look after them."

"I think I wouldn't like that," Rania said frankly. "Why, you'd have no freedom at all."

Hattia stopped scrubbing to stare. "Freedom? I was free to choose Lothril. Now I'm happy to make friends with his mother and help her. We get on very well."

Was Hattia's position any different from hers? Sandwriter was training *her* to be her successor in the same way that Lothril's mother was training Hattia. Yes, there *is* a difference, she decided. Hattia chose Lothril and his family, knowing what she was getting into. I never chose Sandwriter.

When work was finished Rania had a quick wash and changed into her red dress, thankful that the weather was still cool enough for it to be comfortable. But spring is coming, she thought suddenly, as she smoothed the dress over her hips. Spring is coming and the five years will be over.

She went downstairs to meet Atbin and together they walked across town to the house of Lothril's parents. The carved door opened directly onto a courtyard with a fig tree growing in its middle, a welcome shade in the heat of the day, now hung with gaily colored lamps. It was packed; the "little celebration" must have had fifty guests. Hattia introduced Atbin and her to everyone and each person bowed to her, almost as if she were royalty, instead of being Methra's servant girl. She found herself responding automatically with the manners she had learned long ago from her mother and Nan.

They sat at long tables set up around the tree, and a procession of tureens filled with soup, platters of baked fish, dishes of smoked pickled fish, bowls piled with fruit and vegetables was brought from the kitchen. Voices rose cheerfully into the night. Only when she spoke, Rania noticed with embarrassment, did a silence fall on the crowd, as everyone waited politely for what she had to say. By the end of the lavish dinner she was almost entirely silent.

When the last figs and dates had been eaten and the table cleared, Lothril got to his feet. His head was bandaged, and he was still a little wan, but he spoke strongly.

"Welcome, friends. Thank you for coming to celebrate our safe return. It was a near thing and I was right foolish. Rania came specially to warn me not to sail with the craybot fleet, because she had seen my death in a vision."

Oh, no! Rania tried to sink down in her chair and become invisible. Beside her she felt Atbin stiffen and she looked at him with a shy smile.

"I was greedy for the craybot profit and I was right rude to her. For which I ask forgiveness now. Well, you all know what the storm was like. Waves like walls of water. The wind tearing our sails into shreds. When I first saw that storm come roaring out of the south, I knew I'd been a fool not to listen. Then the mast cracked and there was nowhere to run to. 'I'm done for and that's the truth,' I thought. All my promises to Hattia gone like sand in the wind. 'If you'll only save me, rain gods,' I prayed in that flash before the mast hit, 'I'll make it up to Rania for my rudeness.'"

He turned to Rania, sitting beside him. "So I ask your humble pardon for being so rude and stupid. There, I've said my say."

He sat down to a roar of applause. Under its cover Basti leaned across Atbin to ask, "How did you learn to far-see, child? Is it something you can do any time you want?"

"I learned it from . . . from a wise woman in the desert."

"Will you do it for me now." Basti held out her upturned palm. "Please, Rania, will you tell me what you see?"

Rania shrank back. "But I know nothing of fortune-telling, truly. What little skill I possess is quite different."

"It won't hurt to look, will it, dear child? I'm sure you have the gift."

"Atbin, what can I do?" she whispered.

"You are her guest. It would be insulting not to."

Reluctantly Rania took the outstretched hand and pretended to study the pattern of lines on it. As she stared, unable to think of anything to say, the pattern faded and she heard her own voice saying, "Your husband will die comfortably in his bed of old age and you will be a grandmother within a year."

The roar of laughter and approval woke her from her dream state and she snatched her hand back as if from a blazing torch. But the damage was done. Now they were all crowding around, hands waving under her nose, voices screaming in her ears.

"Me next."

"Read mine, do!"

"Mine, mine!"

The more she refused, the more desperate they were to share in her gift. Reluctantly she looked at a few more hands. She said things, anything. Looking around, she caught Hattia's eye.

"It was a wonderful party, thank you. But I must go. I'm so tired."

"Of course. I'll get my parents and tell Atbin you are ready to leave. But . . . just before you go . . . please, for me."

"Not you, Hattia. It isn't right. It's not what I was trained to do. It was just an accident."

"No, it's a gift. A wonderful gift. Surely you won't be selfish, you'll share it with a friend."

With a sense of dread Rania took Hattia's hand in hers. It happened as before. The lines faded and she heard her own voice from a long way off. "You and Lothril will marry in the next twenty days. You will have a son . . ." With an enormous effort she forced herself to hold back the words.

"Well?"

"Well, what?"

"You didn't finish. You were going to say—"

Rania shook her head. "I'm sorry. It's gone, whatever it was."

Hattia glowed and looked almost beautiful in her happiness. Rania had to turn away from it. She was trembling and afraid she might faint. She took Atbin's arm as they said their final good-byes and left.

The night air was cool and the breeze was off the desert, with a tang of zaramint on it. Rania had a sudden desperate longing to be alone, totally, completely alone. She thought of the cave and the quiet drip of water into the pool. It was a long time since she had thought of it.

Wrapped in the turmoil of her thoughts she didn't really notice Atbin's unusual silence. He knocked at the inn door. It swung open. Methra must have been waiting for them.

"Was it a good party? How tired you look, my girl. Off to bed with you. Atbin can tell me all about it."

Upstairs, Rania tore off her red dress and washed herself from head to foot, feeling as soiled as if she had fallen into one of the drains that carried the filth of Monar down to the sea. But she could not wash away the memory of what she had done.

She thought of Sandwriter and of all the others who had been Sandwriter before her. Women going back to the beginning times of Rokam. Women who, each in her turn, had taken in one hand the terrible power of the rain gods and in the other the gentle secret of Roshan that lay in the dark cave. Power in one hand, wisdom in the other. Passed on from woman to woman down through the ages. Like a river running through Time. Flowing forever unless it was dammed by a woman who refused this terrible gift. Or who misused it.

As she had done.

"Never again, I promise. Never again."

"How was the party?" Tekla asked as they scrubbed the tavern floor, next morning.

"A big crowd. And Basti made a splendid feast. Then Lothril thanked me for— Really, it was silly. He owes me nothing."

"I can see the rich food disagreed with you." Tekla laughed, but left her in peace. But as they did the laundry Hattia told Tekla about the fortune-telling.

"Hattia, don't. I should never have—"

"But it's a great gift. Tekla, she told me that—"

Rania put her hands over her ears.

"Now see what you've done, silly. You've dropped the end of the sheet in the dirt. What's the matter with you? Lothril's safe in spite of your gloomy predictions. You're famous and popular and Atbin is in town. You should be on top of the world!"

"Sorry, Tekla. Give me the sheet and I'll rinse it out."

As soon as the laundry was done Hattia hurried

off. As Rania went toward the kitchen Tekla caught her arm. "Don't go."

"What is it, Tekla?"

"I was wondering . . . would you . . . please?" She held out her hand.

"Not you, too! Oh, Tekla, think. The future belongs in tomorrow, in next year. Today is the only place where you can actually live. And you could spoil all your todays worrying about tomorrow if you knew what it would bring."

"Not me, especially if you give me a lucky future."

"But it's not mine to give. Believe me, Tekla, I know—"

Tekla snatched her hand back. "You didn't say all that to Basti or Hattia and the others, did you? You were glad I was your friend when you were nobody, but now I'm not good enough."

"That's just not true. Tekla—" But she was talking to the empty courtyard.

I've got to get out for a while, she thought, and ran through the door into the crowded street, still in her work dress and wet apron. She walked blindly, without thought, until a familiar voice stopped her.

"Hey, Rania, what's happened to your red dress? Not tired of it already?" She found she was standing by the dress shop, whose owner leaned over to smile at her. "You shouldn't come out in that old dress and apron. You've got your reputation to think of."

Reputation? What did the woman mean?

"I've got a lovely dress here. Straight from the Far Isles. Just look at that embroidery. Beautiful, isn't it?"

"It certainly is. But I could never afford it and I don't need another."

"I wouldn't *charge* you, dear. A gift. Just tell everyone where you got it. And, if you'd consider . . ." She held out her hand, palm upward, across the counter.

Rania shook her head violently. "I can't— I'm sorry—" She ran along the lane, around a corner and down another street, until she had to stop, out of breath.

"Hello, me dear. Where's your friend Tekla?" The baker of sweetcakes was leaning on her plump arms over the counter.

"I just ran out for a breath. It's crowded this evening, isn't it?"

"Always so after the craybot catch. I've been frying cakes all day. Try this one, it's new. Dates in the middle."

Rania held up her empty hands.

"That's all right. You're an old customer. Tell me what you think of it."

Rania bit through the crisp coating to the fluffy dough and the sweet center. "It's delicious. Should be a best seller."

She had turned, deciding she must go back to the inn before Methra missed her, when the baker called again. "Don't go, dear. There was something I was wanting to ask you."

"Yes?"

"Well, it's my eldest son, Jestil. He left home four years ago to be a sailor. Just a lad, and I haven't seen or heard from him since. They say the boat sank, but I don't know, do I? Maybe he went ashore before it happened. I could bear it if I only knew. It's the not knowing that wears a body down."

Rania stared at her in wordless dread, knowing what her next words would be.

"They say you've got the gift. If you could just tell me what's become of my lad."

The mouthful of sweetcake turned to sand in Rania's mouth. She managed to swallow it somehow. Gently she put her hand over the baker's. "What you've heard . . . it's exaggerated. I don't have that kind of gift . . . I'm sorry."

She ran, throwing the rest of the cake into the drain as she turned the corner. She scrubbed her fingers violently on her damp apron.

"Where've you been, my girl? There's work to do."

The tavern was packed and the dining room filling up. There were platters to scrub and tankards to rinse.

"Lord, what a day!" Methra wiped her forehead as she bolted the door at the evening's end. "If this goes on I'll be able to retire in ten years! Rania, don't go yet. I must talk to you, my dear. There's been people in and out all day, leaving little gifts for you, flowers and candied fruit and I don't know what and all. I've put them up in your room. Oh, I've heard the stories. What a sly one you are, to hide a talent like that! Anyway, I've made a plan and I want to discuss it with you, private like."

"Oh, Methra, I'm so tired. Can't it wait until morning?"

"You may sleep as long as you choose in the morning. There! What do you think of that? I've decided that it's just not fitting for a person with your gift to be scrubbing and doing the laundry and—"

Rania stared, "But I've been glad to earn my keep."

"And so you shall. Just sitting at a small table in a corner of the dining room every evening—I wouldn't have you in the tavern, it wouldn't be fitting, but the dining room is nice and quiet."

"Whatever for?"

"Just to let my guests talk to you, show you their hands, maybe. What do you say?"

"Oh, Methra, not you, too?" She burst into tears.

"What do you mean? It'll be a grand thing for business. If things go as well as I plan, I'll cut you in for a share of the profits. Maybe a tenth. You'll be set for life, my girl. What do you say to *that*?"

"I couldn't. Not possibly. I'm not a fortune-teller."

Methra's mouth tightened. "It wouldn't matter if it didn't always come off, would it, dear? You just tell them what they want to hear. It'll be true often enough to keep them coming. No, I'm not going to let you give me your final answer yet. You sleep on it and think about a tenth of the profits of the Fair Wind and not having to turn your hand to the heavy work ever again."

At last Rania was free to run up to her room. Even here she was not free of the memory of this disastrous day. Methra had not exaggerated. Her bed was laden with gifts.

What *am* I to do? she wondered. She pushed open the eastern window to get more air into the room and saw a familiar figure strolling up the street toward the inn. Atbin. He would help her put this nightmare behind her and make everything all right again.

She ran quietly downstairs to open the door before he should knock and bring Methra out of her room. She slipped out and left the door ajar behind her.

He wasn't expecting her and his initial reaction was one of shock. Then he drew back and bent as if to kiss her foot. Bent as he had done when he left the offering baskets at the handar. As if she were someone special. Someone different.

"Atbin, it's only me. Rania."

His laugh was forced and he did not meet her eyes. "Rania. Yes. I have been hearing such stories all day. I didn't know that *she* had taught you such power."

She shook her head. "It's not a power I want. It's terrible, a mistake."

"How can the work of Sandwriter be a mistake? She holds Rokam in her hands."

"*She* does. I do not. I'm a woman, Atbin, who once long ago was a princess. Who once long ago was apprentice to Sandwriter. I'm neither of these things now."

He didn't hear or else he chose to ignore the pleading in her voice. He knelt suddenly and kissed the hem of her dress. "You are as far above me as the stars, lady," he whispered. Then he slid past her into the inn, leaving her standing by the door, listening to the revelers down the street.

10

*T*he inn was asleep. All except for Rania. She moved quietly around the attic room, making her preparations. Her clothes were neatly folded, together with a note saying: For Tekla. They could divide her rejected gifts as they saw fit. The thorn-wood doll. She picked it up and held it tenderly for a moment. But it was the gift of a sixteen-year-old youth to a little girl. Neither of them was the same person today. She laid it back on the chest.

She had put on the desert robe that she had worn on her journey to Monar the previous spring, almost a year ago. She had twisted the coppers she had saved into a kerchief and tucked them in the girdle of her robe. She would need the money to pay for a kroklyn and hoped it would be enough.

She didn't really worry though. Since she had seen Atbin outside the inn it seemed that she was no longer in charge. The rain gods had neatly removed every choice from her and she had only to do as they commanded. What could go wrong as long as she followed where they led?

"You can sleep as long as you like," Methra had said. So her room would be undisturbed until noon, at least. By then she would be too far to follow. So long as Methra did not suspect . . . and suspect she would if she found the front door unbolted in the morning.

Rania looked out of the south window. It was a not long drop to the roof of the next-door house and from its sloping roof to the ground. She would never manage the climb in her full desert robe though. Quickly she stripped it off, rolled it into a bundle with her money in the middle, tied it with the rope girdle and tossed it into the street outside.

I was naked before, she remembered. When Sand-writer took off my robe and cut my hair I was reborn into my life as an apprentice. Then I had no choice. This time it is I who choose.

She climbed over the sill, wriggled around and slid down until she was hanging by her fingertips. She dropped lightly to the roof tiles of the neighbor's house, let herself slide to the edge, and again dropped. She stood, shivering in the cool night air and looked for her bundle. There it was, gleaming white in the starlight. She dressed quickly, tucked her money into her waistband, and set out for the kroklyn stables.

Monar slept under the stars. Rania moved like a shadow on her bare feet through its dark streets. Due east until she encountered the city wall, she reminded herself, and then north until she came to the stables. They were not hard to find. The acrid smell of kroklyn made her nostrils wrinkle while she was still two streets away.

She recognized the place at once. The only danger now was in waking up a perfect stranger. She bit her lip, wondering how to go about it. But she needn't have worried. A small boy slept against the wall under a flickering torch. Obviously a guard. She shook him awake gently.

"Get Rathbin for me. It is urgent." He looked at her with wide, sleepy eyes. "Do you understand?"

He nodded, scrambled to his feet, and pattered up a set of stairs that led to a gallery above the stables themselves. She waited patiently and at length he reappeared with Rathbin in tow, the latter tucking shirt into trousers as he came.

"You are . . . Atbin's friend, aren't you? What is the matter?"

"I need a kroklyn to get to Ahman."

"Tonight? A caravan will be leaving in little over a day."

Rania shook her head. "I have to go now."

"You are asking for Atbin's new beast? Why doesn't he come for it himself, and at a decent hour of the day?"

"No, I don't want Atbin's beast. I want to hire a kroklyn for myself. To cross the desert *now*." In spite of her belief in the rain gods Rania was growing impatient. Time was going by. In a few hours it would be daylight. She must be far away by then. Too far to follow.

"I do have a gentle beast, fit for a lady to ride," the young man said slowly. "But —"

"Thank you. I'll need five days' supply of mishli and water, and food for the kroklyn. And a blanket."

"Can you truly handle a kroklyn?" The young man ran his hand through his tousled fair hair.

"Yes."

"You got gloves?"

"No. I'll need them, of course."

"You surely will. Your hands'll be cut to shreds without them. You'd better hire a driver."

"Have you got one?"

"Not until the caravan goes the day after tomorrow."

"Then I'll go alone."

"It's madness. You'll get lost."

"That I will not. I know the stars and the desert is my friend." She spoke with authority and could sense him beginning to yield.

"What if you're wrong? What if you die in the desert?"

"I don't intend that to happen."

"These are my father's beasts. They're expensive beasts to raise and train. Suppose *it* dies."

"You're quite right. I will leave you a note. If anything should go wrong you will be repaid. Have you paper?" She hesitated, after he brought a piece of grubby paper and a very old quill pen with a worn nib; then she dipped it in the ink bottle he held for her and wrote:

> Dear Grandmother,
>
> If you should receive this I will have died in the desert. I will have died true to Sandwriter and what she has taught me. Please pay the bearer what I owe him.
>
> Your loving granddaughter Rania.

She folded the paper and wrote *"Lady Shudi, Lohat"* on the outside.

"Here." She gave it to him, together with her coins.

"This wouldn't pay the rent of a kroklyn to the first oasis, much less to Ahman, lady," he said, tossing the coins in his hand.

"What can I —? Yes." She slipped the pendant over her head and handed it to him. The stone was warm. Red with gold dust caught in it. Her love gift from Atbin. The last thing that was hers. "Will it do?"

"I'll saddle a beast and bring it out. With food and water for *six* days and a blanket. Wait here."

He opened the stable door and slipped inside. The rank, warm smell of kroklyn was overwhelming. She could hear him rousing one of the beasts. It bellowed in complaint, a shockingly loud noise in the silent street. Above her head a shutter was pushed open and a head peered out.

Rania crouched in the shadow of the gallery. The shutter banged close again. Rania looked anxiously at the sky. Already the midnight constellation was in the western quarter. It would not be long before dawn broke. The little boy, who had been staring at her curiously, went back to his post beneath the lamp and curled up on the ground.

At last Rathbin reappeared, leading a laden kroklyn. He forced it to kneel. "Here's a pair of gloves might fit. Wear them all the time, mind. If he gets a smell of water he'll be off and the reins'll cut your hands to shreds. D'you need a hand up?"

"I must do it myself, thank you. There'll be no one out there to help me."

"True enough."

She stood on the beast's folded front leg, grasped the thick hair on its neck with both hands and hauled herself into the saddle. She crooked her right leg around the saddle horn and felt for the stirrup with her left foot. Not waiting for her to settle, the kroklyn's head whipped back so that its red eyes stared straight into hers. Its teeth gleamed and it hissed menacingly.

Rania looked steadily back. "All right then," she said quietly. "Off we go." She grasped the reins and dug her left heel into its flank. Slowly the great beast lumbered to its feet, rear legs first, so that she pitched forward onto its neck, and then the front legs, so that she had to grasp the saddle horn to avoid sliding off the rear.

"That's well done." Rathbin sounded less worried. "Fare you well. May the gods protect you."

"Thank you. I believe they will. You are doing the right thing, so do not be concerned. Good-bye."

Rania did not look back as the kroklyn moved off. She took the eastern gate and immediately turned south. Before long she could feel, beneath its soft footpads, the beaten path that lay, as straight as a bee's flight, across the desert to the first oasis two days' journey away.

Two days, she told herself. Or a night and a day, if I can stay awake that long.

It was evident that Rathbin had chosen the kroklyn for reliability rather than speed. It kept its head to the faint trail and plodded steadily onward. Rania checked their path against the stars. She could follow that bright cluster until dawn. Once the sun rose she would have to watch the sand itself to make sure they did not stray from the trail.

It did not seem long at all before the first faint glow

appeared in the eastern sky to her left. She whispered the prayers of welcome to the sun and had just completed them when it leapt, a brilliant red ball, into the sky. The kroklyn trudged on.

Rania investigated the panniers hung on either side of the saddle. She found a leather water flask and a cake of mishli. She broke off a piece of the gray mass and ate it thoughtfully. It was tasteless and insipid compared with the spicy food of Monar, but it was nourishing. She washed down its dullness with two careful swallows of warm water, tasting of the leather flask.

The sun turned gold and the kroklyn's shadow became a harsh black shape against the brown sand to her right. The kroklyn plodded on. Now, in the monotony of the desert, there was nothing to keep Rania's thoughts from crowding to the front of her mind. Methra, hands rubbing together, jolly eyes gleaming at the thought of her profits . . . The dressmaker, palm outstretched, demanding . . . The people at Basti's house, their palms turned to her, their lives opening inside her mind, all the pain, the greed, the fear and hope.

There were the others. The baker of sweetcakes, her face shadowed with worry for her missing son . . . Hattia dreaming of her marriage to Lothril, of her son . . . Tekla, whom she had refused.

What could she have given these people if she had

stayed in Monar? Would she have told them lies and false promises? Or the truth? The truth that the baker's son was a thief, languishing in a foul prison in northern Kamalant. That Hattia's desired firstborn son would die of the redspot before he was two?

She thought also about Atbin. Her last memory of him was the cruelest, as he bent to kiss the ragged hem of her work dress, his eyes no longer full of friendly admiration and love, but of awe.

The sun beat brutally upon Rania's head and shoulders. She pulled her hood forward over her head and loosened the girdle about her waist, so that the robe fell freely from shoulder to ankle. Her skin felt harsh and her lips dry. She half closed her eyes against the glare on the sand. The kroklyn plodded on.

At sunset she made the kroklyn kneel, which it did most willingly. She slid to the ground and hobbled the beast with a line from the bridle to its rear ankle. Then she squatted beside it on the hot sand and inspected its footpads, dislodging a small stone that had stuck between two of its toes.

She mixed a gruel for the kroklyn in a pannikin that Rathbin had provided, and only after it was fed did she sit, with her back against its hairy side, and eat her own small meal of mishli and dates, washed down with two mouthfuls of water.

"How beautiful the desert is," she said aloud. "Beautiful and harsh. Like life, I suppose. Hattia's son will die, but she will have had the joy of a son for two unspoiled years. And the baker will have the memory of her son as a boy, unspoiled by the knowledge that he will die in an alien prison."

The meal over, she climbed stiffly back into the saddle. This time the kroklyn did not hiss as she mounted. Perhaps it was getting used to her, or perhaps it was grateful to her for taking the stone out of its foot.

The sky was dark and the southern stars beckoned. The desert track ran directly toward them. "How wonderful it will be to be among the stars, to be part of the Great Dance. I wonder how many stars there are, kroklyn. More than I can count. Perhaps there are more, far off, that I cannot even see, just as I cannot see the palm trees of the next oasis."

In her mind Rania saw the Great Dance of the stars about Rokam as but one small portion of a dance so vast that no human could begin to understand it. So vast that it must be beyond the ken even of the rain gods. "I wonder who made that Great Dance. How splendid those gods must be!"

Overhead the stars wheeled by like a great clock, marking the divisions of the night. The kroklyn plodded on. Rania's head nodded and she dozed. The stars faded and the sun flushed the eastern sky.

Shortly after sunrise the kroklyn let out a piercing scream. Rania jolted awake and clutched the reins.

"Easy. We'll be there soon enough," she soothed the thirsty beast.

She stared ahead and saw a shimmer of light to the south. She licked her lips and raised her head. *Water. Or mirage?*

She let the kroklyn have its head. The wind blew back her hood so that her hair flew free. She was on the back of Freedom, galloping around the palace paddock, a ten-year-old with every worldly joy in her hand, loved and spoiled and safe.

Only a day later and it had all been taken from her. No path across the desert could take her back to that happiness. There was no way back to the only place she could truly call home. Tears ran down her cheeks and dried salt in the wind.

She brushed her hand across her suddenly blurred eyes and cried out in surprise, because directly ahead of her were the tasseled palm trees of the first oasis. They had arrived.

Once the kroklyn was watered and tethered close to a grove of zaramint bushes where it might comfortably graze, Rania stripped off her robe and slid into the stone bath beneath the date palms. She gasped as the water stung her hot skin. Then she lay, half submerged, her hair floating around her like black seaweed, until she was almost asleep.

Reluctantly she climbed out, slipped on her robe over her wet body, and lay in the shadow of the bathhouse, sleeping dreamlessly until she wakened in the late afternoon. She walked about the small oasis, working the cramps out of her legs, picking berries and watching with amusement the small desert snakes that skimmed across the hot stones as she approached and the sand-colored lizards, running spraddle-legged up the trunks of the date palms.

She had eaten snakes and lizards, she remembered, on her first desert journey nearly five years ago. A child of the desert, the drivers had called her, when she enjoyed their food. Tasty as they were and tired though she was of the continual diet of mishli, she could not now take the life of even a snake or a lizard.

The kroklyn seemed to be in good condition so, as soon as the sun had set and the first stars appeared to confirm her direction, she mounted once more and continued on the trail that led southwestward toward the oasis of Ahman. Toward the Great Dune. Sandwriter. And her destiny. It would be three days' journey with no shelter but the open desert. If she and the kroklyn could stay awake she might make it in two nights and a day.

It was pleasant riding at night, knowing that the waterbags were once more full, feeling her skin cool and freshly washed under her loose robe. The kroklyn, too, seemed to move with a more eager stride, perhaps knowing that its own stable lay far behind and that to go ahead was the better choice.

At dawn came a short rest, as the stars faded but the light was not sufficient to see the trail. Again she looked carefully at the kroklyn's feet. They were her life, as much as the bottles of water, so carefully rationed.

The sun rose and it was possible to discern the faint line across the otherwise featureless desert. To an untutored person there *was* no line. But Rania had spent five years learning to see. From the kroklyn's back it was clear, a faint sheen that differed from the untrodden desert.

This was the road to Ahman. If she should stray far enough from it to be out of sight of the red mountain and the Great Dune at the end of her journey, she would ride on and on until she and the kroklyn dropped and gave their bodies back to Roshan, so that one day, perhaps, a traveler might see a cactus or a thornbrush growing green through their bones.

Shortly before noon Rania saw a thin dark line along the southeast horizon. It looked like a mountain range. Only there *were* no mountain ranges. Fear clutched her chest as she realized that in that dark line lay, not just a faint possibility, but the likelihood, of death.

By noon the wind was blowing in hot metallic gusts, like the heat from a blacksmith's furnace. The sun hung huge and copper-colored overhead. The kroklyn whined uneasily. Rania rose as tall as she could in the saddle and scanned the land around them for the possibility of shelter, however slight. A bush would do. Or a rock. But there was nothing.

She rode forward as fast as she dared, hoping to find some kind of shelter before the storm struck. Now the sky was tinged with copper and the sun had almost disappeared. Sand stung her cheeks. She turned the kroklyn, so that its left flank faced the oncoming storm, and signaled for it to kneel. It complied willingly and at once buried its head in the shaggy hair beneath its stomach.

Hastily Rania got out the blanket and a small amount of food and water. She spread the rug on the ground against the right flank of the kroklyn, pulled her hood forward and wound the loose scarf around her face so that there were only two narrow slits left, one to see and the other to breathe through. Then she squatted on the rug, her back against the kroklyn's flank, and pulled the blanket up over her head and down between her back and the kroklyn to make a small secure tent.

The wind came like a swarm of angry bees, carrying the desert on its back. She could feel the sand hitting the blanket above her head in a continuous vicious bombardment. It was stiflingly hot, growing hotter every minute, and she had to battle the temptation to fling back the blanket, tear the scarf from her head and gasp in fresh air. She had to keep reminding herself that outside there was no air, only a boiling mass of sand and dust, suspended on the wind, which would instantly fill her mouth, her nose, her lungs.

The sweat trickled down her back and armpits. In the darkness the wind screamed and the sand pounded over her head.

"I was a fool to leave Monar," she said bitterly. "I had friends there. I was respected. Only a mad person crosses the desert alone."

She remembered the day when the unbroken kroklyn had run away with Atmon. If Sandwriter had not sent the rainstorm he would have died that day, experienced in the desert though he was. "Shall I call on Sandwriter? Shall I ask for help? What did she say once? 'The balance of Rokam.' No, I won't upset the balance of Rokam. I will wait and see what the rain gods have in store for me."

She felt worn out, heavy, as if the weight of the whole of Roshan were on her shoulders.

"But it *is*. The sand is above my head, weighing me down. The kroklyn must be completely buried. Suppose it's too deep for me to dig my way out? Then I'll become part of Roshan, that's all."

It felt like Sandwriter's thought, as if she were closer than Rania had suspected. Comforted, she ate a few crumbs of mishli and took a single sip of water. Then she slipped into an uneasy doze.

She woke, stifling, with no idea whether she had been asleep for a few minutes or a day. Her blanket cave was darker than the darkest night. Outside was an impenetrable silence. Only the dead weight of sand upon her head and shoulders told her that she was still alive, still feeling.

She tried to struggle to her knees, but the weight was too great. She tried swaying to and fro, hoping to dislodge the sand, and finally felt a sudden release of pressure. She pushed upward, got to her knees and then to her feet, the blanket falling to one side.

She stood up to her thighs in sand. When she turned around she could see only a small dune that had not been there before. It was nighttime, dark and starlit. She could see not further than ten paces or so.

Where was the kroklyn? Frantically Rania began to dig into the side of the newly formed dune. Her fingers felt thick hair. A saddle strap. One of the panniers. The sand slithered back as fast as her hands could move it. She fumbled blindly inside the pannier and found the kroklyn's feeding pannikin. Using it as a scoop she hurled sand away until the leeward side of the beast was exposed. With careful fingers she brushed sand away from its head, still buried in its stomach hair.

Was it dead? If it was, then so was she, a night and day's ride from Ahman. She put a trembling hand against its side and felt the slow, deep drumbeat of its heart. It was sound asleep.

"Wake up, you lazy creature! Up!" Her voice was

high with relief as she slapped its side. Dust rose in a choking cloud.

The kroklyn poked its head up. The small red eyes looked around. It sneezed lavishly, rolled onto its knees and shook itself. Mounds of sand slithered down its windward side.

Rania shook the sand from its eating dish and mixed a meal of mush. While it was eating she checked her supplies. Enough food and water for two extra days if she was careful—and she was accustomed to being careful. She unwound the scarf from her face and shook her hair loose. Then she climbed into the saddle, gathered the reins, and called on the kroklyn to get up.

From the height of the saddle she could pick out in the starlight the new features of the land caused by the raging wind. Dunes had formed against any interruption in the land, a crack, a thornbush, even a pebble. They would not last, these storm dunes, but for the moment they changed the landscape.

The trail, of course, was gone. All she had to guide her were the stars at night and the sun by day, and the latter was a poor guide, since it moved so fast from east to west the traveler would tend to travel in a westerly direction also. Low in the sky Rania could just discern the star cluster that had been her guide. She pulled the reins and turned the kroklyn in that direction.

When the stars faded she let the kroklyn stop. They

had made poor time during the night, as the poor beast had to wallow through the windblown sand rather than on a well-traveled trail. She fed him and herself, shielded herself with the blanket, and tried to sleep.

The sun set in a welter of crimson, orange, and gold, as if the gods had splashed half the rainbow across the sky. Once it had faded Rania looked anxiously for her stars and set out again.

Two nights. The third should bring her into sight of the red mountain. But she woke during the third day to find that they were trapped in a maze of dunes, star-shaped, ridged, all reshaped by the storm. She could see where long-standing tufts of desert grass were almost buried.

She climbed to the top of the highest dune and looked around. A sea of dunes, like a frozen tempest. She was close to panic and forced herself to take a slow, deep breath. "This has happened to me before," she said aloud and began to remember.

She looked around again. This time she could see patterns in the chaos. She could see that the wind had shaped the dunes in one direction. South must be over *there*.

She knelt by a patch of sharp desert grass, felt beneath the drifting sand to the packed sand below. Dug in it with her fingers, feeling for the underground root that must lead to the parent plant. That way. She walked on to the next plant and dug again. It was like a series of dots that joined together, formed a line. The line pointed toward water, toward the great underground reservoir that showed itself in the secret cave of the red mountain at the heart of Roshan.

"Come, kroklyn, time to be off." She climbed stiffly into the saddle and urged the beast to its feet. Slowly she walked it along, her eyes steadfast on the tussocks of grass. She had indeed come too far west.

After a time she noticed that the desert plants were beginning to grow more closely to each other, sometimes no more than ten strides apart. The kroklyn twitched its nose as if it were smelling the promise of water. They rounded a dune and Rania saw, in the distance, the red mountain.

Rania dismounted a little way off and hobbled the kroklyn. She walked across the burning sand toward the cliff face, noticing that a particular thornbush was in bud, that over there a cactus had begun to flower. Winter was over and spring had come.

It was late afternoon now and her shadow rippled black over the surface of the rocks as she walked toward them. She looked up. *There* was the entrance to their cave. She climbed up to it, her tired legs aching. Her shadow was swallowed in the cave's shadow.

She stood in the entrance, waiting for her eyes to adjust from the glare outside. In the darkness something moved. A face upturned, eyes brilliant.

"I have just made soup and there is fresh bread," Sandwriter said.

"I am very hungry"—Rania hesitated and then went on firmly—"for everything you can give me."

"That is good. Come and eat."

The two moved toward each other, the old woman and the young girl, and embraced as equals embrace.

ABOUT THE AUTHOR

*M*onica Hughes is one of the most popular
writers for young people and has won numerous
prizes at home and abroad. Her books have been
published in Poland, Spain, Japan, France, Scandina-
via, England, and Germany. She has twice received
the Canada Council Prize for Children's Literature
and was runner-up for the Guardian Award.

She is the author of *Keeper of the Isis Light*, an
American Library Association Best Book for Young
Adults, which also received a Certificate of Honor
from the International Board on Books for Young
People; *Hunter in the Dark*, also an ALA Best Book for
Young Adults; and *Invitation to the Game*, among
many other titles. *The Promise* is the sequel to *Sand-
writer*.

Monica Hughes was born in England and now lives
in Canada.